THE
O'MALLEY SAGA

Book Two:
Thunder Mountain

THE
O'MALLEY SAGA

Book Two:
Thunder Mountain

•

TOM AUSTIN

AVALON BOOKS
THOMAS BOUREGY AND COMPANY, INC.
401 LAFAYETTE STREET
NEW YORK, NEW YORK 10003

PRINTED IN THE UNITED STATES OF AMERICA
ON ACID-FREE PAPER
BY HADDON CRAFTSMEN, BLOOMSBURG, PENNSYLVANIA

I would like to dedicate this book to my maternal grandparents: my grandfather, the late Thomas L. Bradbury, who taught me the value of honesty, hard work, and loving the land; and my grandmother, Leola R. Bradbury, a full-blooded Bohemian, and a full-blooded lady. She taught me to love family, bake apple pies, grow gardens, and swing on a bag swing in the hay barn.

Acknowledgments

As with many endeavors, this book was a cooperative effort. My sister and fellow author, Merry Austin-Adams, is also my personal editor. I thank her from the bottom of my heart for her help and encouragement. My wife, Karalee, keeps me based and makes me continue working until I get it right. It's been a wonderful marriage, and she's lucky to have me. (I guess that's one man's opinion.) My agent, Kristen Lindstrom, who is long-suffering, patient, and destined for sainthood. Thanks for the hours. Marcia Markland, my editor and one of my biggest fans. I thank her for making me feel like a real "American Hero." My readers and fans. Richard Heap, Kim Peterson, Brice and Wrendee Henry, my mom, my kids, Larry, David, Bob and Maxine Behrendt, Bishop Dan Olsen, Keith Broadhead, who is my friend and the best mayor the world has ever seen, and all the others who I know have actually read what I have written. Thank you. You make me want to get on with the third book. I want to know what happens just as much as you do.

Chapter One

I smelled their dust and heard their voices 'fore I saw 'em. I was glad I'd left my horse up on the back side of the ridge that loomed behind me. Sin, bein' the friendly critter he is, would've surely nickered at the other horses. One sound from either me or my horse and trouble would have been on me.

I'd walked and slid down a steep slope into the thick stand of aspens looking for an ornery cow with a spring-born calf. I'd seen her headin' up this direction a few days before, and a cougar would surely enjoy a meal of calf. The trees was too thick to ride through, so I'd been walkin', slidin', and fallin' over downed quakies. I'd just fallen again and was climbin' back to my feet sayin' unpleasant things under my breath when I smelled the dust. I stopped dead still, barely breathin'. Then I heard 'em. They was close, maybe only twenty or thirty feet from me.

I stood motionless, glad I was screened from the trail by a giant blue spruce. I reached down slow and easy, checkin' the .44 Army in the holster to make sure it was still there. The wooden grips were cool and smooth under my hand. I took a single step deeper into the branches of the tree and pulled one down a tiny bit. I could just see the mountain trail through the cover of spruce needles.

The Injuns were ridin' single file on the narrow path that climbed to Carnreo Pass. They was painted and wearin' feathers. I could tell they weren't Utes 'cause the paint weren't right.

I stood dead quiet, hardly breathin', watchin' the Injuns pass; then I heard a voice come driftin' down from toward the front of their column.

"Beck, it's going to be dark in a few hours." The voice was

raised to be heard over the rattle of rocks and thumpin' of hooves on the trail. ''Watch for a place to camp.'' The man's voice didn't sound like an Injun, and it carried a ring of command. I slowly turned my head back to look at the braves that were still ridin' past and involuntarily sucked in my wind.

She was pretty, dark-haired, and her hands were tied to the pommel of the saddle. She was wearing a blue calico dress, and they had her ridin' astraddle a big horse. She turned her face toward me as her horse stepped over a rock. She was young and tryin' to be brave, but I could see the terror in her eyes and etched in lines on her face. She passed behind the aspen trees that lined the trail, and I lost sight of her. Two more braves rode past close together, and the last one turned his face toward me just as the girl had done. I almost jerked back, but I knew movement would give me away quicker than anythin'.

He stopped his horse with a jerk on the rope he was usin' for a bridle and looked right at me. It was like he'd noticed somethin' a little out of place. My hand tightened on the Army gun, and I felt sweat break on my forehead. He shook his head slightly, then kicked his horse in the ribs. With a single lunge, the horse and man disappeared behind the trees that lined the trail. I let out my breath, waited for a slow count of ten, and then moved. I found a spot in the quakies where I could see them, but they couldn't see me. It was quite a sight watchin' somethin' over twenty painted Injuns work their way up the slope. My heart was surely in my throat, and I kept an eyeball watch on the trail behind 'em in case they had a rearguard out. I heard hooves on the trail below comin' up at me like the last pack had done, and I melted back into the aspens.

I hunkered over and did a sneaky, slow walk for a spell 'til I figured I was out of sight, then I took out at a dead run up the hill for my horse, makin' as little noise as I could. I'd seen enough. They had a girl with 'em, and I knew right where they were gonna camp. There was only one likely spot on this side of the pass. I had to get to the ranch. I had to get some help.

I made the ridge, suckin' wind and slobberin' down my chin. I mounted my black horse, turned his head back toward the game trail that I'd followed over from the ranch, and held him to a fast, quiet walk until I was well away. I pulled my stirruped feet out away from Sin horse and kicked him solidly in the ribs. I wasn't wearin' spurs, but he just weren't used to me kickin'. He near unseated me as he took a jump that whipped my head back, and with a snort he settled into a neck-stretchin' run.

Sin loved to run, near as much as he liked a good fight. I'd gotten him from a former Union general that had 'most hung me over a simple misunderstandin' during our time in Kansas a while back.

I hated bringin' trouble with me down out of the hills 'cause we already had enough problems. The partnership had decided to move the herd west from Kansas last fall instead of waitin' for the spring. We wanted to have our spring calves on the ranch instead of havin' 'em along the trail and losin' maybe half. We'd taken a gamble, and with the way of gamblin', we'd lost. Me and Mike had stayed on the ranch site, waitin' for the cows. I'd been shot up some in a little fracas and wasn't up to much anyhow. The rest of the crew pulled into the valley in middle December, just in time to be caught in a five-day blizzard. They'd lost some critters along the way, and the rest of the herd was stressed 'cause of the travel. By the first of the year, we was lighter on the count by some two hundred head. That was just the beginnin' of it. We'd had a long, heavy, and hard winter without enough cut hay stored by. Fact was, by time the thaw come around, we'd lost near half our herd, and the calf crop hadn't made up the difference. I knew we was in money trouble, and I hated bringin' more difficulty to my family and friends, but there was no help for it. The captive girl needed help, and we were all there was.

Sin and me made good time, and I found a way over the summit without going through the pass. When we broke out of the timber into the big long meadow that led to the Storm King Ranch, I let the reins go slack, and the black horse stretched out in a sprint.

The Storm King Mountain lay behind me now as did Carnreo Pass. We called the flat-topped mountain Storm King 'cause every time a storm come up, it seemed to gather right at the summit. The Utes called it Thunder Mountain, and with good reason. I seen times during the early spring when the lightning was almost constant at the rocky crest. We'd named our new place the Storm King after the mountain.

I come foggin' into the yard, pulled my Colt's Army from the cut-down cavalry holster, and touched off a shot in the air. A few minutes later most of the men had gathered 'round me.

"Where's Mike and Owen?" I asked, not seeing my older brothers.

"Mike headed to Fort Lewis to see if they wanted more beef. He left right after you, early this morning. Owen is over in the meadow," The Major replied.

Mike had lost an arm in the war, but he was still as good a cowhand as you'd find anywhere. The Major, Major Bob Daly, had been with us from the beginnin'. In fact, the Major had been with my brother Owen durin' the troubles with the Jayhawkers before I ever met up with them in Kansas. He was the leader of the partnership we had formed, and natural born to it.

I saw a movement from the corner of my eye and turned to see Owen slidin' from his horse near the barn. I started talkin' as fast as my mouth would move.

"I spotted a pack of Injuns on the south side of the pass. They had new hair on their lances and a woman captive." I stopped a minute to catch my breath and then continued. "They wasn't Utes nor 'Shones, and I heard one of 'em say they were gonna camp before they come over the pass. He was talkin' good English. I think he might've been a white man."

The Major's hand went to his chin. "Might be the renegade band that Ignacio and Ouray were telling us about," he said. He turned toward the rest of the men, "Wedge, get the Colt revolving shotgun from under my bed and bring my rifle. Tony Rabbit, get the gray horse from the corral for Matthew and rub Sin down. Walk him a bit before you turn him out to the pasture. He's been hard used."

Tony Rabbit was one of the Ute boys we'd hired from the Southern Ute tribe to help us with the stock. His name wasn't really Tony Rabbit, but we couldn't pronounce his Injun name, and it surely sounded somethin' like Tony Rabbit.

"Owen, how many of those bark cylinders of Matt's are left?" the Major asked.

"Probably a half dozen," Owen replied. He looked thoughtful a minute and then glanced over at me. "That's a good idea. I'll get three or four of them."

We'd been havin' trouble keepin' the elk out of our haystacks, so I'd made up some cylinders from willow bark, filled them with rifle powder, fitted a couple of ends on 'em, waxed 'em up good with beeswax, and stuck a hank of cannon fuse in a hole I made with my blade. Dependin' on the length of cannon fuse you could make 'em go off a spell after you lit 'em up. It give the elk time to get to the stacks 'fore they blew. They didn't hurt nothing, but they made a powerful lot of noise, and scared the elk all the way back over the hill. We might find use for something like that before the night was over.

I slipped to the ground and peeled the saddle off my lathered horse. I rubbed his neck a second and he looked back at me. There'd been times when I reckoned the big black horse was nearly the only person that liked me, and I had some strong feelin' for him. He'd never let me down.

Tony come back leading the gray and took Sin toward the corral.

Wedge come a runnin' from the house carrying an armload of guns. Watching Wedge run was an event in itself. He was the biggest man I'd ever come 'cross in my life, and he was the best friend I had, next to my brothers. First time I'd seen him I figured he was over three hundred pounds and only a little of it fat. He'd once had a nasty habit of tearing folks' ears off, but he hadn't done that for a spell. He was smaller now, since the ranch work had made him lose some of his belly. He was probably down to two-ninety-five. His arms were as big as my legs, and he could throw a half-growed steer all by hisself. I watched him pass the guns over to the Major and looked to my own.

My Henry, in the boot on my saddle, was loaded to the gills, and I had three extra loaded cylinders for my Army.

"Vic," the Major yelled at the top of his voice. Another young Injun boy came running from the barn and slid to a stop in front of the Major. "Vic, I want you to catch up three fresh horses. Ride one of them and lead the other two. You head for Fort Lewis as hard as you can. Switch horses when the one you're riding gets tired, and don't stop for anything. Get Mike and the soldiers heading back this way. Tell them we have trouble here, and they must hurry." The Major paused a moment and took a deep breath. "Do you understand, Victory?"

"Yes," Vic replied and turned for the corral, running as he left. The other men were at the lodgepole corral ropin' horses and slingin' saddles on 'em. The air was full of dust, noise, and confusion as we gathered the things together we'd likely need.

"Mount up, boys," the Major hollered, just like he'd probably done when he was pushin' his cavalry against the Union troops.

I looked back over my shoulder at the peeled log cabin we'd put up. It was only three rooms right now with a bowed roof, but we'd left places to add other rooms as needed. Durin' the summer most of us had slept either in the barn or out under the stars, 'cause the cabin just weren't that big.

I been kinda hopin' I'd need my own cabin 'fore much more time went by. Lee, my girl, had stayed in Denver City to run the eatin' house that the partnership had there. I'd reckon most folks would say that me and Lee had us an understandin'.

The partnership had done some investin' out in Abilene, and the Major had run an eatin' house back there on the Kansas plains. He'd made a good go of it, 'cause he was a powerful good cook. Men had rode for miles just to eat one of his fruit pies or some of his pastry, and the same thing was happenin' in Denver City. The money from the eatin' house and selling culled beef from our remaining stock was all the money we had comin' in.

The Major had lately come out to the Storm King to help us move the cows back down to the ranch meadows from our high-country summer range, and Lee had stayed in Denver to run the eatin' house. Owen had come out from Denver with the Major, and he'd brought his wife, Patty, with him.

Patty was Wedge's sister, but looked nothin' like him, which was a blessin'. Her and Owen had gotten double hitched back in Kansas, and it surely looked like they was gonna make a lifetime matched pair. Patty was lookin' from the door now, and I gave her a wave and a smile. She waved back but didn't smile. Wedge had told her what we was up against, and she was some worried.

"How far from the pass were they, Matthew?" the Major asked, bringing my thoughts back to the Injuns.

"I'd guess they was five miles from the big meadow before you begin the climb to the summit. Time we get there, they should be lookin' for a place to pull up and camp."

There was six of us. We'd hired three hands over the summer, and they was good help. One of them, Christian Silva, was a local valley Mexican and a good hand. I reckoned him to be a good man in a fight, even though I'd never had the chance to see him shine. Something 'bout him made me think he might be quick, and his gun was hung to the front, close and handy on his belt. He never said three words, but was always there pulling his weight.

He'd had a hard time of it. Folks mostly weren't kindly toward Mexicans, but they'd been in the San Luis Valley a long time 'fore the Anglos were. His father come from one of the richest families in either New Mexico or Colorado Territory. Chris come out to us 'cause he wanted to be away from the influence of his family and learn the cattle business our way. There was also some rumor that he'd killed a man down in Taos. We didn't pay much attention to that, and there weren't nobody gonna ask him. A man's business was his own, and as long as he did his work, nobody much cared what happened at Taos. Chris was loyal to the O'Malley brand, and in the short time he'd been with us, he'd near become one of the family.

The other two men, Price and Sanders, were drifters that showed up together looking for a few weeks' work and had stayed on for a few months. They were good men, but we reckoned they'd head for Denver City come first snow.

We rode quiet and fast, makin' time in the meadows while we could 'til the trees started closin' in on both sides, makin' a funnel that led us to the Carnreo Pass trail. We started climbin' up toward the pass, knowin' that the renegades was just on the other side. The Major, who was at the front of our company, pulled up and waited for us to gather 'round him.

"Where do you think they are, Matthew?" he asked me.

"I'd say they're below the pass in the meadow just where the heavy timber meets the grass."

The Major stepped out of the saddle as did the rest of us.

"It looks like it's about an hour until dark. As soon as it gets dark, we'll move forward and try to get in positions to attack when they get to sleep." He stopped a minute and looked right at me. "Matthew, you're probably the best woodsman among us. I want you to start now and scout their camp. Work your way down until you are positioned reasonably close to the captive." He was quiet a moment, looking at me intently. "I don't need to tell you to be careful. If you are discovered, it not only puts all of us in jeopardy, but they will surely kill the prisoner." He turned from me as I handed my reins to Silva.

"*Señor,* you watch the hairs on your head," Christian said to me.

The way it was supposed to be said was "You mind your hair, ole hoss." It was a mountain man sayin' that we threw at each other now and again, but Chris could never get it quite right. I knew what he meant.

"I reckon," I replied with a grin. I walked back to my saddlebags and took out a pair of Ute double-soled moccasins. After I changed my boots for the mocs, I walked around the back of my horse and took a rough-cut, lightweight buckskin shirt from the other bag. I changed my faded red one for the buckskin, and I started up the trail at an easy lope. I reckoned the renegade camp was a little over a mile up and then just east off the trail in behind the mountain.

The trail was steep, but I'd been spendin' a good bit of time in the high country, mostly on foot, so I was in fair shape for climbin'.

I kept a good pace 'til I figured I'd made half of the distance, then I took to the brush. Injuns wasn't always particular 'bout puttin' out a watch, but they was notional. No sense takin' a chance of bein' seen before I'd even gotten in close. I stayed parallel to the trail, but the brush was thick and slowed me some. It was heavy twilight before I got to the summit of the pass. I went down the south side pretty fast 'til I found the spot where they'd taken off the trail, then I followed their sign in toward the meadow. 'Bout ten minutes of slow walkin', and I stopped dead in my tracks. I could smell woodsmoke, so I was gettin' close. I crawled in under the low-lyin' limbs of a big fir and listened for a spell. After my breathin' slowed, I crept forward and looked out of the screen of limbs. The sun was down, and it was near dark. The sun's reflection from the far side of the world made the clouds a rosy pink, and there were stormclouds comin' up from the west that were a dark purple-blue. It was real purty, but I was hopin' them stormclouds would come right over us and really cut loose. I could see the fire plain. They was 'bout a quarter mile down the slope from me.

I started creepin' down on all fours just like I'd watched a cougar-cat do on our herd one time. I surely hoped I didn't end up like he did. I'd shot him right through the earholes, and his tanned hide was on the wall over my bed.

I crawled a hundred yards, then lay flat and still just waitin'. Pa had told me once that movement was what gives any critter away when they was sneakin'. Man's and animal's eyes pick up movement quicker than anything. He told me to watch a white-footed mouse when a hawk flew over. He'd sit just as quiet as he could 'til the hawk had flown off. Them that moved was the ones what got ate.

I was just gettin' ready to start creepin' again when I heard a deep sigh come from the tall grass in front of me. It was close and made goose jiggers start up my back. It might be a deer, but more likely it was an Injun. I parted the grass and took a look. I didn't see nothin', so I scooted forward a foot and stopped.

Suddenly, he stood up right in front of me, facin' toward the camp. I eased the Toledo steel knife from the fringed sheath on my belt. She was a big knife with a foot-long blade that I kept sharp enough to shave with. I figured to get to my feet real quiet, then it was one step and a quick thrust.

I got the standin' part done just fine. I took a quick step forward and realized I didn't want to kill this man. A friend of mine once told me that the ability to make decisions was one of them things that separated us from the critters. I rolled the knife over and give the man a smart thump behind the ear. I grabbed him as he fell to keep the noise down.

I got down on my knees again and moved toward the camp. I reared up a little and could see the campfire plain. They had her tied to a stump on the other side of the fire from me. She still looked game, but scared. I was gonna have to get closer. I got my feet under me, bent way over at the waist, and started pickin' my way slowly toward the camp. In less then an hour I lay just outside the circle of light given off by the fire. The renegades was crawlin' in under the blankets havin' ate their beans. The storm had moved off to the north, but the rumble of the thunder could still be heard. I could see the girl plainly, but she lay on · the far side of the fire between two big Injuns that surely looked like Paiutes. The other men had the look of half-breeds, maybe crossed between Utes and Navajos. I reckoned the Major was right. They must be the renegades that we'd been hearin' 'bout. No self-respectin' Navajo would ever been caught in company with a Ute. The two tribes just naturally hated each other. The renegades was mostly men and sometimes women that were outcasts from their own tribes. From where I lay, the ones I could see all looked plum mean, and they was well armed.

I had a tactical problem, as the Major would say. The girl lay on the other side of the fire, and I just wasn't gonna get any closer. I figured to wait and see what the Major was gonna do before I moved. I had surprise on my side, and I was close but just not close enough. I looked around the camp again, then back at the girl. If I'd been a swearin' man, I'd have surely come up with some good ones as I watched her. She had one hand free and was workin' on her leg ties with a knife so dull it wouldn't have cut soft butter. I started sweatin' like a new-branded pig watchin' her saw away at the ties. I wasn't breathin', knowin' that all the Injuns couldn't be asleep. They hadn't been down that long.

Heck of it was that she near got away with it. She got the hide cut, and was makin' her way toward me when one of the Paiutes sat up and looked over to where she'd been layin'. He let loose a grunt that sounded like someone had kicked him in the gut, and I shot him. He flopped onto his back, and the big fella on the other side was instantly on his feet.

The girl was out of the camp and come runnin' past me. I shot the other Paiute through the brisket. The .44 ball holed him, but he kept on a-comin'. He fair had me worried as he come at me, and the rest of my shots sounded like one constant blast. Finally, he fell over backward onto the fire, dead before he hit. With the man layin' on the fire, it got dark and confusin'. I dropped the cylinder out of my Army and throwed another in. I started workin' my way backward, but watched my front.

There was a flurry of shots from the far side of the camp, a volley of heavy shots, and then a tremendous blast as one of my bombs went off. That would be the Major and the rest of the boys makin' music, whilst me and the girl hauled out of the area. Trouble was I didn't have the girl.

I turned and started makin' tracks back up the hill. I saw her skylined a second as she made the ridge top. I was four long steps behind her and gainin'. She was makin' hard work of gettin' through the brush in the dark. I caught up to her and grabbed her from behind. That might have been one of the biggest mistakes I'd made in a while. I was all a sudden bein' beat, flogged, stomped, and flailed by a little gal that didn't weigh half what I did. I finally got hold of her and whispered in her ear.

"Settle down, gal. I'm your friend. We're here to get you out."

She calmed some, and I could see she was catchin' her wind.

"What's your name?" I whispered. I 'sposed if we was gonna die together, we might as well get friendly.

"I'm Jessie May O'Flannery," she replied.

"I'm Matthew O'Malley, late of Kansas and now of the Storm King Ranch down on the flat on the other side of the pass."

I saw her eyes get big, and she took a little breath in. "Matt O'Malley, the gunman?" she asked.

"I got a gun," I said.

"We heard about you and your clan over in Denver City. They say you're a magician with a short gun and can shoot the eyes out of flies on the wing with a rifle."

"I'm a fair shot with either a short gun or rifle, but nothin' special," I said. "There's even been times my brothers have out-shot me." I wanted no name of being a gunman. I'd heard tell of some of the boys down in Texas makin' quite a thing over shootin' other folks. I wasn't lookin' for that kind of reputation.

I heard somebody thrashin' around in the brush behind me and reckoned the outlaws were startin' to look for Jessie.

"You keep the mountain on your left side and head for the trail," I whispered to her. "I'll be along shortly."

I got to hand it to her, she never said yeah or nay, she just taken out for the trail. I turned and waited on the man comin' up the hill. I squatted down in the sage, and held my breath 'til he come even with me. I stood quick, grabbed him hard around the chest, and threw him back down the hill. He bounced a time or two, screamin' as he went, but I didn't stop to watch.

I ran like I hadn't run in quite a spell. Probably since the time the she-bear had chased me 'round a fallen pine when I'd got between her and her cubs. I ran 'til I hit the pass trail, and then I kicked it up a notch and kept on runnin'. I was gettin' fair winded, and I was slobberin' down my chin again.

I didn't let up none. I weren't scared, but I surely liked the feel of the night wind rushin' past my face. I heard hoofbeats comin' up the trail behind me, and I stepped off behind a big rock. My heart was hammerin' so hard that it was jarrin' my vision, and I was suckin' wind, but trying to do it quiet. They come down the trail, and I could see their shapes against the sky. They was wearin' hats. I hadn't seen no hats on the Injuns, so I figured they was my folks. I stepped out into the trail, and Chris come up with my horse. I threw myself in the saddle.

"She's with me, Matthew," I heard Wedge yell, which answered my first question 'fore I'd even asked.

''Run, men. They'll be comin' after us,'' the Major hollered. ''We have to get to the ranch, so we can put up a defense.''

He didn't need to tell me twice. I was already in a runnin' mood.

Chapter Two

They come on us just as the sky was turnin' pink in the east. There was more of 'em now than there had been up on the mountain.

"Looks like they found some friends," Owen said quietly, putting my thoughts into words.

"Must be near forty of 'em now," Wedge replied. "The new ones look like 'Paches."

No one needed to tell us what that meant. The closest help was over at Saguache town, and only four or five families there at the most. The Army was a long ways out, and there was just no way we could hold out against forty determined braves for very long.

We'd put the shutters down with slots cut in them for a rifle to fire through. I looked again and felt a deep sigh come up and force its way past my lips. If it wasn't for the fact that the warriors riding slowly across our hayfield meant to kill us all, the spectacle would have been downright purty. They was mostly on a skirmish line with their weapons held down close to their horses' necks. It was late in the year, and the mornings were cold. The steam from the horses' noses left little puffs of fog hanging in the air.

"We might be a little short handed, but we can give them hell when they hit us this first time," the Major said. "We cost them enough maybe they will quit."

"Yeah, and maybe it'll just make 'em mad," Price said.

"Make every shot count," Owen said. He had the front door open just a crack, watchin' as the renegades and Apaches come across the creek.

The women had turned over the heavy slab pine table and had several boxes of shells torn open. Jessie and Pat both knew how to load our pistols, so they had caps, powder, and ball close at hand. Jessie May also had the shotgun close about her. If the Injuns breached the door she'd make 'em pay.

I heard a high-pitched scream coming from the front and looked to my rifle slot again.

"Here they come," the Major yelled.

I picked up a target over my sights but held my fire. They was still a ways out, and I wanted to make the first shot count.

"There's a few on foot on the backside too," I heard Wedge say. "Looks like they mean to hit us from all sides."

I wondered if I'd ever get to hear Wedge and Owen sing the wonderful songs they'd learned over the time we'd been together. I looked around the inside of the cabin quickly, and I thought of Lee. Young men always have dreams, and I'd surely had my share. Lee and I'd spoke of havin' a big family full of boys, with a girl or two thrown in to take the edge off the boys. I wanted to live. I wanted to see what my life would bring.

I heard a shot from the other side of the room, and then the air was full of shots and screams as they closed on us. I shot careful and saw the man I'd been aimin' at thrown from his horse. I changed my view and took another man as he made a fast turn in front of me. I swung to the side and missed a shot at a brave with a big stomach who was running toward the cabin with a tomahawk in his hand. Owen shot a second after me and knocked the man down. He got back on his feet, and I fetched him with a good shot. I swung to the other side and realized that the main charge had carried past us. Price was firing as fast as he could from the north window as they rode past, and both Wedge and Silva emptied their guns at the back side of the cabin.

"I need a rifle," Owen yelled as his firing pin clicked on an empty cartridge. Jessie threw him a gun, which he caught in his right hand. He swung around just in time to shoot a brave running up the steps of the front porch.

"We got about half of them on foot and the other half as cavalry," the Major yelled.

A rifle barrel appeared at the edge of my vision, and I stepped away from the shutter. The man snuck up quickly and stuck his gun in the slot. I grabbed it and pulled as hard as I could. The rifle went off, but I'd pointed it toward the ceiling. There was a loud satisfying thump on the other side of the shutter as the Injun's head connected with the cabin wall. The rifle came loose in my hand. I pulled it inside and dropped it on the floor. My ears were ringing from the deafening noise of the shots and howls, and I could barely see in the interior of the cabin for the powder smoke.

I heard one of the women scream and looked toward the south window. The puncher named Sanders was down on the floor, and a hand with a pistol in it was pointing straight at me through the slot in the shutter. I heard a tremendous blast, and a huge hole was blown where the pistol had been. I looked toward Jessie, who still had the Colt shotgun to her shoulder with smoke curlin' from the barrel. She'd surely saved my bacon.

Suddenly, it was quiet.

"Get loaded," the Major said. "I saw most of the ones on horses drop off into the tall grass along the canal, and I'd bet the ones that were already on foot are lying close about."

I stuffed shells into my Henry and made sure my Colt was close to hand. I looked back into the room and saw our force had been cut down. Price was shot high through the right shoulder and had a burn across his forehead. Sanders, on the south, was dead. Wedge had a mess of slivers from the shutter stuck in his face, and Silva had a bloody hand.

I hadn't been hit, nor had the Major and Owen, near as I could tell. I counted five bullet holes in the plank table the women were behind. The shots had come in through the front window slots and the door, and must have been near misses on some of us.

I looked from my firing slot into the growing light of the morning. There was a mist rising from the canal we'd dug to bring water from the creek to our irrigation pond. It was a beautiful morning with the smell of death close about. I counted five Injuns down in front of us, and I knew there was a few more in the back. We hadn't trimmed 'em down much.

I heard a single shot from the back, and then heard Wedge give out with a mild cussword. I knew he'd missed. They'd be some tougher now. They'd come fast and disappear quick as they worked their way closer to the cabin.

"They plan on getting in close before they make the next rush," the Major said. "Try to mark where they drop down and keep watch on just that one spot. When they jump up to run again, put them down for good."

It was advice from a man who'd spent some time fightin' the Osage in Kansas before the war.

I kept my eyes peeled to the front and suddenly saw a thin and fast brave jump from the grass and run toward the cabin. He took me by surprise and dropped from sight just as I triggered the shot. I knew I'd missed him clean, and I marked the spot he'd fallen. I saw other movement from the corner of my eye, but I concentrated on the spot where the skinny guy went down. Again, with a rush, he came runnin' toward me a little to the right of where he'd fallen the first time. I swung the Henry slightly and squeezed her off. He stopped, took a single step forward, and fell loosely in plain view.

They kept it up for the next hour, and we notched only one more, but fired probably over twenty times between us.

All at once they came up together as if on a signal. They were runnin', screamin,' too close to us and too many of 'em. I heard the other men in the cabin shouting and shooting. I fired until the Henry was empty and dropped it to the floor. I grabbed my pistol, turned to look at Owen by the front door, and shot a brave just as he made the porch. There were at least ten more behind him. Owen slammed the door and dropped the bar down. He staggered to the table, gave me a stricken look, and fell. Pat screamed, and the women dragged him into the relative protection behind the table. Jessie came back up with the Colt revolving shotgun in her hands and a deadly look in her eye. The door buckled as they hit it, and they spilled through. I emptied my pistol, dropped the cylinder out, and was knocked from my feet. I heard Wedge let out with a tremendous battle cry and jumped back to my feet. I reached up and grabbed a brave's arm as he swung a war ax at

me. I broke his arm as I jerked the ax free and fetched him upside
the head with the ax. I turned toward the rest of 'em. I saw red
and black as the old rage poured over me, and I waded in scream-
ing at the top of my lungs. I swung right and left in great swift
arcs with the war ax, and men fell away in front of me. I looked
quickly around the room and saw Price movin' toward the front
door with his pistol smokin'. I saw a spot of red appear on his
chest. He stumbled and fell to the floor, surely dead. I turned
toward the door and immediately saw a man I knew by sight.
The big bulk of Macon Beck, one of my blood enemies, filled
the door, and he had a pistol pointed right at me. I headed for
Beck on a dead run, howling with fury and ignoring everything
else that was going on around me. I saw panic come up in Beck's
eyes as I gained on him, and he spun around in the doorway
headin' back out the way he'd come.

A very lithe and fast man come at me from the right side
holding a big knife down low. He stopped a few steps to my
front where I could see him plain. I wanted Beck, but I'd have
to take care of this fella first. He was white. He was even dressed
as a white man, but had an Injun headband on and his face was
painted. It fair took me by surprise, him being white, and he
nearly got me with a wicked slash 'fore I recovered. I countered
his slash with the battle-ax and backed away. He come after me,
fast. I stepped aside as he rushed past, but he swung the knife in
an arc as he did. He cut me wide across the arm and chest. It
burned like fire, and bled some. He turned quickly and come
again. I feigned weakness, and he took the bluff. He stepped in
close, and I got my left hand on the forearm of the hand that held
the knife. I swung the ax, and he ducked his head just an instant
before I would have taken it off. The momentum of the swing
drove my strikin' arm down, and he jerked free.

I knew he had me, and he knew it as well. I had one chance.
I didn't swing my right arm up to recock it the natural way. I
simply brought it up from the floor in a back-hand swing. I caught
him as he was comin' in on me. The ax took him right alongside
his head. It did some terrible damage to the side of his face. He
backed away from me, stunned.

I took a step forward to try and finish him, but I was gettin' wobble-kneed and had slowed some. He stepped back and shook his head like a wounded panther.

He looked right in my face, and I realized he had blue eyes and blond hair. He was young, slightly shorter than me, and maybe thirty pounds lighter.

''You've scarred me, O'Malley'' he said simply. He shook his head again and touched his hand gently to his face. I saw fire and hate come into his eyes. ''We'll meet again, you and me, Matthew O'Malley. No matter where you go and no matter how much time and distance separates us from this moment.'' He stopped talkin' a minute and took a deep breath. He looked right in my face, with naked malice jumping from his eyes. ''I'm Nathan Kurlow, and I swear by my blood and yours that you'll die.''

I stupidly looked down and saw that the blood falling from both of us had mingled on the floor of our cabin. I looked back up, and Nathan Kurlow was gone. It struck me then that he'd called me by name.

I turned back toward the fight, which had moved to surround Wedge. Silva was down, lying with his face against the wall unmoving. He was either dead or wounded. The Major was down but crawling forward toward Wedge on his hand and knees, trailing blood behind him on the floor. Jessie had reloaded the shotgun and nearly deafened me with a blast at a man that was runnin' out the front door. Wedge was down under three Injuns, and I ran clumsily toward him. I swung right and left with the ax, clearing two men off him. He scrambled to his feet and smashed the remaining man with one of his giant fists. I threw him my knife, and we turned back toward the door.

They were gone. I fell to my knees with my hands on the floor and sucked wind into my tortured lungs.

I heard it then. The beautiful music of the United States Cavalry. I looked up just as the men rode in perfect order past the cabin chasing the renegades and 'Paches back toward the mountains. There were scattered shots, some shouts, and then quiet.

''Get stood up here and let me look at ya,'' Wedge said. He

helped me to my feet and walked me to the door. "You're certain gonna need Patty to put some stitches in ya. He opened ya good."

"You saw him then?" I asked.

"I did. I saw Beck as well." Wedge replied. "Maybe the Army can tell us what white men is doin' leading a pack of renegade scum."

"He knew me, Wedge. The one that cut me knew my name. His name was Nate Kurlow." Wedge looked at me strangely and then walked me toward the door.

I looked out across the hayfield and saw a man riding a horse toward us. He was wearin' the blue of the U.S. Army and had the gold of a captain on his shoulders. There was something strangely familiar with the way he sat his horse. I went weak in my knees again and started to go down. Wedge tightened his grip on me and kept me standin'. The man on the horse had the bearing of a veteran Army officer, and his Cavalry hat was pulled low down over his face. He stopped his horse in front of us.

"This man needs immediate attention," he said, lookin' at me and talkin' in a voice I instantly recognized. "I have a man with me that's good with wounds. I'll have Sergeant Murphy bring him around."

"Danny," I said almost to myself. "Captain Dan O'Malley, you've come home. I finally kept my promise to Pa."

I started seein' bright spots, and, all of a sudden, I was layin' on my back with my brother Dan standin' over me.

When I woke, I was layin' in the shadow under the porch roof that came only in late afternoon. My chest and arm felt tight and hot, and my head felt like it was gonna float away. I heard a meadowlark over by the river, and then the gentle whistle of a mountain bluebird. I turned to look, and Danny's Army boys was layin' out bodies in a row against the hill across the meadow.

"You been gone awhile, boy," I heard Wedge say. I turned to look at him, and he was sittin' on the porch bench grinnin' at me.

"Owen?" I asked the question with a voice that sounded like the croak of a new spring frog.

"Your brother, Dan, took him and the Major over to Garland

in a wagon. Pat went with 'em to do the nursin'. Them and the ten troopers that were with Dan all headed for Garland.''

"How bad?" I croaked.

"Owen looks tolerable bad. Took a rifle bullet through the upper chest and an arrow into the back. We think he might've caught the arrow early in the fight and broke it off so we wouldn't see it. The Major has a vicious wound in his forearm that broke the bones, and he has a deep knife cut in the thigh that looks like it made bone. He was nearly bled out. He was unconscious when they left.'' The big man was quiet for a moment watchin' the men across the meadow doin' their work. "Price is dead. Shot in the chest," he said.

"I seen Macon Beck shoot him," I replied, quiet like. "I was goin' after him when Kurlow took me on."

"Sounds like him. Weren't Beck involved when your ma was killed?" Wedge asked.

"His brother, Falcon," I nearly whispered. I don't know where Macon was, but he might've been there."

I'd killed Falcon Beck, Macon's brother, and fulfilled a blood oath I'd made on our farm when my mother had been killed by Southern irregulars toward the end of the war.

Wedge reached over and got a dipper of water from the bucket. He held it to my lips and I slurped it down. "Patty kept loadin' all the way through the fight," he said, "and got a bullet burn under her left arm that also burnt her chest. Mighty close thing, that was.''

I looked down at my naked chest and could see the knife cut was puckered up with stitches. I looked back up at Wedge.

"You got more stitches in you than a Sunday quilt. That Army doc and Pat cleaned it out with some whiskey and then commenced to sewing. They did it quick but neat. Doc says you'll live, but you'll be a mite uncomfortable for a week or so." Wedge paused and shifted his position on the bench.

"Saunders was killed; Silva got a dent in the head, and he's seein' two of everything; Jessie lost the little finger on her right hand to a knife, and she has a pretty bad powder burn on her forearm from the shotgun blowing the side out of the cylinder.''

He turned his head and looked toward the cabin. There was a tenderness in his face I'd never seen before.

We watched the boys diggin' holes for a spell and Wedge spoke again. "The Injuns lost fourteen. All of 'em was killed by us in the cabin. They plan on buryin' Sanders and Price under the big ponderosa tree on the left side of the meadow." Wedge ran a hand over his face and looked at me. "They gonna put the Injuns right at the edge of the clearing 'bout fifty feet from the cowhands."

"Seems like a sight of hurt and killin'," I said, with most of the croak gone from my voice.

"Yep, and I reckon one of these days this country will be just like some of them back-East cities. They'll have sheriffs and police to help protect folks. 'Til then we got to do for ourselves, or move back where it's safe."

I knew he was right, and I'd even said something like it before, but it made me sick to think of Owen shot and maybe dyin' and all the others that were hurt or dead. I tried to sit up, and Wedge come over and helped me. I was feelin' as puny as a newborn foal and leaned my back against the cabin wall to help hold myself up.

"Well, good to see you finally got up off the floor," a girl's voice said, close by. I turned and looked as Jessie May came out of the cabin. She had a white bandage on her right hand where she'd lost the finger, and I could see the powder burn was blistered and dotted with imbedded powder. She was holding her right arm up about chin high with her left arm. "If I keep it up like this it doesn't hurt as bad," she said. "I drop it down I can feel my heart beating." She walked toward me and sat down at the edge of the porch with her legs dangling over the side. Suddenly, I saw her shoulders shakin', and I heard little squeaks comin' from her. I looked over at Wedge, but he weren't no help. Neither of us was much of a hand when it come to a cryin' female. I scooted over to her slow, favoring my stitches, and laid my big paw on her shoulder. She reached up and touched my hand without lookin' at me.

"I lost everybody when they hit our wagons," she said in a tiny voice. "I got no place to go, and no one that cares."

Wedge got to his feet and walked over beside us. "You got a place with us, Jessie May," he said. "For as long as you need."

"He's right, Jess," I agreed. "We have need of willin' hands. You're welcome here with us."

She smiled so big it was like sunshine comin' from behind a cloud, then she turned and hugged me. It hurt some, but I figured to suffer through it. She stood and got a hold of Wedge in a big hug. I thought he held on to her longer than was needful, but maybe she was feelin' weak.

We watched as the men lowered Sanders and Price into the graves with ropes. They had 'em wrapped in blankets and lowered 'em real slow. When they got the cowhands all the way down, they stepped back and the bugler played taps. The music lifted sweet sad notes into the mountain air, and I found my eyes were waterin' my chest. I felt sorrowful bad about them two boys. They hadn't been family, but we'd shared meals and coffee together, swallowed the same dust, shared the hard work of the ranch, and they'd died standin' and fightin' with us.

The Army men, already had the renegade graves dug, and they made quicker work of puttin' 'em down. They was more respectful than I thought they'd be, but they didn't waste no time and didn't play taps over 'em neither. They'd made up an armful of rough wooden crosses, and they pounded 'em in at the head of each grave. Sanders and Price had their names and the date of their death carved into 'em. When the Army got done and had left the little graveyard, I looked at them crosses and hoped that there wouldn't be any more added anytime soon.

"My head hurts like I have been drinking the tequila from the bottle," Chris Silva said as he walked through the door of the cabin.

"You got a fair bump on your noggin." Wedge looked up at the graceful dark man. "Good thing you Mexicans are so hardheaded."

Chris snorted as he tried not to laugh. "Do not make me laugh, *señor*. It causes me pain, and I might have to shoot you."

"We got anybody fit enough to keep a watch?" I asked, thinking about the morning fight and the chance they might come back.

"Mike is over behind the barn. He come back with Dan." Wedge paused a moment and looked over toward the blue-uniformed Army men who had gathered by the barn taking care of their stock. "From what I hear, Mike met Dan and his boys on the trail over to Fort Lewis. Victory showed up shortly after, and that hurried 'em along some. They was in company with this troop from Lewis," he said with a nod of his head toward the troopers.

"Dan says he went back to Fort Leavenworth to get out of the Army awhile back, but one of the generals talked him into stayin' on awhile longer. Seems he's workin' on somethin' special. He has five handpicked men with him. From what he says they was all with him during the war." Wedge fell silent, thinkin' a minute about what we'd been talkin' about. "The boys down there," he continued with a gesture of his hand again toward the Army, "are troopers from Lewis. They got a lieutenant in charge of 'em. They come out to check on word that there was some renegades makin' trouble."

"They got a firsthand look at 'em." I said.

Wedge nodded and then pointed toward the creek. "Tony Rabbit is over in the creek brush watching toward the north. Victory is watchin' the stock. The Injun boys hid out in the trees 'til the fireworks was over just like the Major told 'em to." Wedge shifted his weight and looked out across the meadow to the front of the cabin. "I ain't too bunged up, so I reckon I can spell Mike tonight, and the Army will be watchin'."

"You think they may come back?" Jessie asked. There was a small tremor in her voice.

"I don't think so," I replied, "but you just never know with Injuns. One or two of 'em might come back just to try for some horses." I was quiet a moment as I remembered some of the things I'd learned since I'd left the farm in Pennsylvania. "It don't hurt to plan for the worst 'cause sometimes that's what you get," I said. I was still pretty young when it come to countin' time, but some of the experiences I'd had over the past couple of years had growed some hair on my backside, and a little on my chest.

"I made some stew and baked some bread if anyone wants to eat," Jessie said as she walked toward the door. I looked up and realized for the first time that Jess was downright purty. She'd combed, fixed, and done whatever it is that girls do to make themselves look good.

"Stay set," Jessie said, lookin' at me from the door. "I'll bring you a plate out." I didn't feel much like arguin'.

Wedge stood and cut loose with a yodel that rebounded from the hills and mountains that lay close about. For a homely man he had the most incredible voice. It was a beautiful sound and pointed up how quiet this place was toward the evenings. Mike come out from behind the barn, waved, and started walking toward us.

We had a quiet meal as the shadows began to get long and the birds started making their sleepy sounds over by the spring. Wedge and Jess walked over toward the end of the porch and ate by themselves, talking quiet. Watchin' and listenin' to 'em made a body feel right lonely. Chris and Mike sat by me, but they wasn't near as purty as Jess. I was sore missin' Lee and decided right there and then that soon as I could breathe comfortable I was makin' me a trip to the city.

I finished eatin', moved a little, and sucked in my wind. My chest hurt like blazes, and I could see that Jessie was fair hurtin' as well. Chris was holding his head and once in a while would shake it tryin' to make his double vision go.

I heard a woof of laughter from Wedge as he looked us over. "This is the worst-appearin' crew I ever seen," he said. I reckoned he was right.

The evenin' wore on and soon the stars started poppin' out one by one.

Jess was sittin' next to Wedge on the porch, and he was singing the lullaby softly, right to her, in his beautiful baritone. I rolled my blankets out right there on the porch floor, and the last thing

I remember was Wedge and Mike singin' a sad Irish ballad about a highwayman.

A slow week went by, and all of us healed some. Jess was a great cook and kept us full of food. Day by day she gathered back some of her spunk, but there was a deep sadness in her eyes. Far as we could tell, she'd lost all her family durin' the past few weeks.

The Army patrol from Fort Lewis headed for the Los Pinos Indian Agency. Los Pinos was about forty miles from us over Buffalo Pass and served the Southern Ute tribe. The men figured they might hear some word on the renegades and 'Paches that had attacked us from the man at the agency.

Word come to us that Owen was havin' quite a struggle and didn't seem to be gainin'. The Major had taken a turn for the worse as the knife wound became infected, and the surgeon at Garland had determined that the bullet wound had shattered both the bones in the Major's arm. He wanted to cut it off at the elbow, but the Major wouldn't let him. He said he'd rather die.

A week and five days after the fight at the cabin, my brother Danny, a full troop of regular cavalry, and Dan's ten troopers come ridin' through the meadow in front of the cabin. They was all turned out in their blues and flying the American flag at the front of their column of twos. When they split off, I saw they was escortin' an Army freight wagon draped with black velvet, and my heart jumped into my throat. Wedge come walkin' up from the barn, and Jessie May come out of the cabin. I could see Mike makin' his way up from the corral at the spring.

I knew what the wagon carried. I just didn't know who.

Chapter Three

" "May God grant this man peace. Amen."

Danny did a right fine job of preachin'. Near as good as some of the sky-pilots I'd heard back home in the farm country. There was tears leakin' from my eyes as I watched the boys lower the flag-draped coffin into the ground. The Major had fought for the Confederacy, but after the war he was an American like the rest of us. He deserved the honor of the flag.

We was standin' under the big ponderosa pine where we'd buried the cowhands after the cabin fight, and now we was buryin' another of our own. The Major was the second man of our partnership we'd lost in these western lands. The Kiowa had been the first, killed by Comanches back on the short grass of the High Plains. I reckoned they'd be walkin' the warrior's trail together now, and it made me feel some better, but not much.

Owen had insisted on comin' out to the ranch for the buryin'. Him and the Major had been together for a spell before I'd come into the picture, so he took the loss hard. I didn't think I'd ever seen him nor Mike cry, but they was both bawlin' near as hard as me as we threw dirt onto the wooden box.

Owen was still mighty puny, so we'd carried him in a chair from the cabin out to our little cemetery. He looked like he was gonna be joinin' the Major right quick if'n he didn't get laid out on a bed. He was in poor shape, and the shock of the Major's death hadn't done him any good. I was scared for him.

"Let's go to the house," Captain Dan said quietly when we'd finished. Wedge and Danny grabbed Owen's chair and carried him gentle as they could toward the house. Me, Mike, and the girls followed 'long behind, none of us feelin' much like talkin'.

27

When we got to the cabin they laid Owen out on a bed careful, and Patty hovered over him. His face was bright with fever, and the pain had set sharp lines around his mouth and eyes.

The rest of us sat down around the table, which still showed the bullet holes from the fight.

"I resigned my commission this morning," Dan said without any warnin'. "I figure my place is here with my family, and it looks to me as if you have need of another pair of hands. Mike's told me about the winter kill on the herd, and I figure you could use another man to help spread the trouble out a little."

Pa'd have been proud of him. Family ties had always been one of the things what drove the O'Malley tribe, and Pa had told us time and again that we was to take up and do for each other.

Dan was quiet for a moment and looked around the table at us one by one. He was the oldest of the brothers and had always had a good head on his shoulders. He'd been promoted from buck private all the way up to captain during the war, and I knew there was a story that went with the promotion.

"I don't have much to bring with me," he said, "about five hundred dollars, and a willingness to work. Maybe it isn't enough. I know all of you have a lot more invested than that, but it's all I have. If you want, I'll work my way into the partnership, making my wages go toward the price." His voice was clear and steady, and I knew him to be a singer like Owen. The Irish was big on singin', but I'd never got the hang of it. Him and Owen and Mike had been quite the thing back in the valley. Come meetin' time, folks would travel all the way from Hog's Holler just to listen to the O'Malley boys limber up their lungs.

"My men are mustering out as well," Dan said. "We've been together so long it would seem strange not to have them with me. They plan on staying here and working for wages if you'll have them."

Somethin' seemed a little strange to me. I knew it weren't all that easy to get out of the Army. I'd heard more than once that deserters were shot, even in peacetime. Danny and his men weren't deserters, but he was talkin' like you could just walk into the commandin' officer's room at the fort and tell him you was done with the Army, and he wouldn't object to it. Somethin' was goin' on, but it wasn't up to me to ask the question.

"Listen," Owen said in a voice so weak it scared me all over again, "I was lying beside the Major when he came awake a few days ago." He stopped and breathed hard, gathering his strength. "He knew his time was short, and he made me promise that we'd give Dan whatever share of the partnership he'd accumulated. Owen fell silent, and I felt the tears well up again. I blinked my eyes 'til they went back down and then looked 'round the room at my brothers.

"That's just like the Major," Mike said in a quiet voice.

"I guess we all know that we was his only family. . . ." I said, my voice sounding strange in my ears.

"It's only right, Dan," Wedge said. "We need the help, and you and your men would be welcome. We'll make that five hundred go further than you'd ever imagine."

We'd all been heard from, and it was the only vote that was needed. Danny O'Malley had come home. It wasn't Pennsylvania, but I reckoned he'd never figured on goin' back to the little farm anyhow. Home's mostly where there's people what care for a body, and Dan's people were here.

"Your men will have to work for grub and hold off on the wages 'til we're better set. We got almost no hard money," Wedge said.

"They already know that and have agreed," Dan replied.

"We got us one more problem," Wedge said. "There's a little gal runnin' an eatin' house over to Denver City that don't know nothin' 'bout what's happened."

I blushed and then felt rotten. I'd been feelin' so sorry for myself, I'd near forgot my girl over in Denver. The Major had hired good help for Lee to ease runnin' the place, but her and the Major had been close. She just wasn't gonna take his death very well.

"I'll head over to Denver in the mornin'," I said. "I reckon it's my place."

"It would probably be best," Mike agreed. "She'd take it better from you than any the rest of us."

I nodded my head in agreement and looked 'round the room. These people were my friends and family, and the brothers was all gathered together for the first time since before the war. Pa would be proud of us makin' our own way in this new land. He'd always been big on that. He reckoned a man had to make his own trail and fight his own fights, and we'd done all of that. We'd done it alone at times, and we'd surely done it as a clan. We was havin' trouble, but we'd face up to it together come what may. I wished Pa could see us.

"We can't send anybody with ya, Matt. Time's gettin' short to get the hay in, and the signs say we gonna have an early and hard winter," Wedge said. "With Owen down, we're gonna need all the hands we got to get the work done."

"My men and I should be of some help to get ready for the winter," Dan said.

"You're gonna get all the work ya want," Wedge smiled. "We got to add on to this cabin, build two or three more, get the winter wood in, get a whole winter's worth of hay in for the herd, put by our food for the cold time, and a world of other things."

"What we gonna do with the Denver eatin' house?" I asked, thinkin' about the things I'd need to tell Lee.

It was dead quiet in the cabin. My question brought us squarely back to the reason we were here. The death of our friend.

"I don't rightly know . . . " Wedge said, his voice trailin' off.

"I don't know the girl that's running it," Danny said, "but maybe she'd want to buy the place."

"She don't have the money, and she's got no family to get it from," Wedge told him.

"I think we should give Lee the place now and let her pay us from the profits if she wants to keep it. Otherwise, we should probably sell it on the open market," Patty said, looking at us seriously. Owen was asleep, snoring gently, and Pat was a full partner since her and Owen had got married. She always had good ideas to offer durin' our business talks. "I think she'll want to sell it," Patty added. "The last time I spoke with her she planned on coming out to the ranch before full winter set in."

She looked pointedly at me. I felt the color come up in my cheeks and ears.

"If'n everyone agrees, we'll leave it to Lee to decide," Wedge said, lookin' 'round the table. Everyone nodded their heads.

It looked like I was headin' to Denver in the mornin'. I could feel excitement start to climb up in my gut. It'd been a spell of time since I'd seen Lee, and I was overdue.

Sleep come hard to me that night, and I was up gettin' my stuff together an hour before daylight.

"You got money?" Wedge asked, as I rolled up my bedroll.

I stood and checked the poke bag tied to my belt. "Maybe twenty dollars," I said quiet, so's not to wake them still sleepin'.

"That be enough to get you there and back?" Wedge asked.

"Shouldn't need much. I don't plan on stayin' long nor buyin' anything more than I need."

Wedge nodded and walked out the front door. I followed close behind, and he helped me catch up my horses. I was takin' both the gray and my Sin horse, so I could make the trip faster. I tied my bedroll up behind my saddle and stuffed some food in my saddlebags.

"Would you get me some of that Union pipe tobacco?" Wedge asked. "I'm near out, and I can't seem to get over to the store at Garland."

"You don't have to go that far for your pipe stuffings," Dan said from the direction of the barn. He was picking hay from his hair as he clamped his hat on, and it was plain to see he'd slept in the big pile of grass hay we'd laid up. "Couldn't sleep in the cabin," he explained. "Too jammed up."

"What ya gettin' at, Dan?" Wedge asked, taking the conversation back to Danny's first remark.

"Man by the name of Otto Mears is putting a store down where Saguache Creek wanders through the flat north of the marsh. He and another man, John Lawrence, are buildin' up that little town."

"Be nice to have supplies a little closer," Wedge remarked. He tied a final knot in the rawhide that held my bedroll on, and looked across the saddle at me.

"Anybody ever tell you what the heck Saguache means?" he asked. We'd had some debate over the question since we'd come into the country.

"Ignacio says it means 'Land of Blue Water, or Blue Springs' in Ute," I replied. "Been called that for quite a spell by the Injuns."

"Mears and some of the other folks over to the town says it means blue earth," Dan added.

"I like the Injun's story better," Wedge said.

"Me too, and it makes sense. The ponds down there by the marsh are blue as can be," Danny agreed. He walked up beside me and pushed his hat back on his head.

"Matt, I wanted to ask you something before you left for Denver," he said. "I was wondering where you got that Winchester sitting in the corner by the fireplace?"

I thought a minute and couldn't place where or what he was talkin' 'bout. Then it come to me. "I had that stuck in my face durin' the fight," I said. "One of the renegades jammed it through the firin' hole, and I grabbed onto it."

Dan seemed concerned as he turned and looked off toward the direction of Buffalo Pass and the Los Pinos agency. "That's a better rifle than the Army currently issues," he remarked. "One of the Fort Lewis troopers found one just like it at Los Pinos as well." Dan turned back toward us and could see the blank looks on our faces in the growing light. "The patrol that left here after the fight surprised the renegades along with some Apaches not far from Los Pinos," he explained. "They were acting like a bunch of poor, starving innocents, and the agent was feeding them. The Army ran them off, and they left a Winchester '66 behind just like the one in the cabin." Dan was quiet a minute and looked at me. "Didn't you tell me there was at least one white man with the renegades when they hit here?"

"There was two. Macon Beck and a younger one that called himself Nathan Kurlow," I said simply.

Dan looked at me sharply. "You sure that was his name?"

"He put the name on hisself during the fight. I fetched him a nasty lick 'longside his head and cut him up pretty bad. He made feud talk 'fore he ducked out of the door.''

''Don't you remember Pa talkin' about the Kurlows?''

I looked hard at Dan, thought for a minute, and then shook my head.

''You were pretty young, but he told the stories so many times, I'd have thought you'd have heard them.'' Danny took off his Cavalry hat, ran his hand over his hair, and put his hat back on. ''We don't have time for the telling right now,'' he said, ''but if Kurlow made feud talk, he meant it. The Kurlows and the O'Malleys have had a blood war going for as long as anyone can remember. It ebbs and flows depending on how strong the families are in numbers. According to Pa, in the old country, if we weren't fighting the English, we were fighting the Kurlows. Pa thought he'd killed the last Kurlow forty years ago.''

Danny fell quiet, and I looked at the light gatherin' on the east horizon. All the talk about Pa made me have a hurt down in my guts again. I missed Pa somethin' fierce, but even more now that the Major was gone.

''One new rifle I wouldn't think much of,'' Dan started again. ''They could have gotten one Winchester during some of their raids. However, it's not likely they'd come up with two. They haven't been on the market that long, and they're expensive to buy. I'd say somebody is gathering up the renegades, and maybe some of the Apaches, giving them some excellent rifles, and using them as a guerrilla army.''

''Nathan Kurlow?'' I asked.

''He seems the likely candidate, but you rarely see the leading man, the one with the money and plans, fighting in the midst of his army. I'd say there's someone else. Somebody with money, position, and power.''

''Well, it's all way up past my head,'' Wedge said, ''and Matt needs to be movin'. It's gonna take him several days to get to Denver City anyhow.''

''You watch your back, Matthew,'' Dan said to me seriously. ''Kurlow obviously won't forget you. There'll come a time when he'll try for you, and it may not be to your face. The Kurlows are a sneaking lot and known for their cunning ways, or so Pa told us.''

"I'll watch, Danny," I replied, disturbed by his words. He seemed to know more, but he wasn't sayin' any more. It was one more part of the puzzle, along with him walkin' off from the Army.

I swung into the saddle, settled the Henry into the boot, and turned my face toward the rising sun. It was a long trip to Denver, and I had a hard bit of work to do when I got there. Lee was waitin', and she didn't know the Major was dead. I wasn't much of a hand at such things, and I hoped I could handle it right. I waved at Wedge and Dan.

It took me most of two days to get to Fort Garland. The fort had been closed, but an occasional patrol from Fort Lewis still used it to stay over. I'd heard that there was a garrison posted at the old fort now because of the Injun raids. The town that had grown up around the fort was still there, and the sutler had stayed on with his store.

I tied off my horses in front of the store, not plannin' on stayin' long, and went in the front door. It was dark and cool inside the store, and it smelled of coffee and gun oil.

"Help ya, mister?" the man behind the counter asked.

"You got a box of shells for a Henry?" I asked.

"Got a box 'round here somewhere. Not many men carryin' the Henrys anymore with all the new cartridge guns around."

"I'm right partial to my Henry," I replied. "I know where she shoots."

"Only one man I know of that shoots a Henry regular. That's Matt O'Malley, the gunfighter. Him and his brothers got a spread over west of here."

I didn't say nothin' as the sutler fished around in a showcase for a box of shells for my rifle. That was the second time recent that somebody had called me a gunhand, and I had no hankerin' for the name. My fights had always been straight up, and I'd either been protectin' myself or some of my people.

A man walked in the door behind me, and I turned to look at him. I didn't like the look of him, nor the smell, either, for that matter. He took to checkin' some canned goods, and I turned back to the store-man.

"There you are, mister," the sutler said as he laid the box on the counter. "That's three dollars and two bits."

I looked at him sharp like. "That's a mite steep, ain't it?"

"They aren't easy to come by, and I don't have much call for them," he explained. "I keep 'em just in case O'Malley decides to come in and needs some."

"Well, get another box, 'cause you're right. I'm the only feller what has a Henry in the country, and you never know when I might need shells to fit it. It depends on how many I got to waste shootin' cheatin' storekeepers."

"You're Matt O'Malley?" His eyes was wide open, and his right hand was kinda twitchin' a mite. The smelly coyote that'd come in after me turned and walked out the door, and I paid him no mind. I pulled my poke bag and counted out the money.

"Thank you, Mr. O'Malley, and come back and see us," he said with a smile.

I picked up the shells with my left hand and hooked my poke back on my belt with my right. I turned and walked back out the door. I was still pretty mad over bein' stuck for the shells, but I needed 'em, so I paid the price. The afternoon sun hit me full in the face, near blindin' me as I walked off the porch and headed for my horses.

"O'Malley," a voice said loudly. I pulled up short and looked off to my right. There was three men facin' me, and they didn't look like they was much on the social graces. One of 'em was the mangy fella that had left the store. I turned slow to face them and they spread out some. It surely looked like gun trouble, and I'd never seen any of these men before.

"I will take the Mexican on the left if you will kill the other two." I didn't look as the voice spoke, but I recognized it as Christian Silva.

"I can probably take all three of 'em if'n you don't want to dirty up your pistol," I replied, not takin' my eyes off the men in front of us. "They don't look like much."

Now that was said in truth. They was a rat-chewed lookin'

bunch, but three of 'em might press me a little. I was right glad to hear Chris's voice close to hand. He'd gone down to Santa Fe a few days after the cabin fight, and I hadn't seen him since.

"What brings you here?" I asked.

"I finished my business in Santa Fe. I stopped to water my horse."

"You sure you want the Mexican?" I asked Chris. "He don't look like he's worth spendin' a ball on."

"Please, *señor*," Silva said. "It is a matter of family honor. The Mexican snake put his hands on my sister. He must pay the price for his arrogance."

Now the men across from us was some puzzled. We was standin' there talkin' about who got who, and they'd plum figured I'd probably be crawlin' and beggin' for my life. They didn't know it, but it just weren't in me to beg nor crawl.

"I think now, *señor*," Silva said softly.

I shucked my short gun and touched her off. The blast was nearly deafening in the quiet of the street. I shot the man to the far right just as he was drawin' from his belt, and then shot the man in the center who had a gun in his hand. I saw the blossom of flame from the barrel of his pistol, but the ball came nowhere near me. I shot him twice more and then turned back toward the man I'd shot first. He was layin' on his back with his arms stretched out. I looked at the Mexican and saw he was walkin' 'round and 'round in little short steps. He fell over on his face, raisin' a little puff of dust when he hit. It was all over in a matter of a few seconds.

I was feelin' a little sick to my stomach. I'd shot men before, but it still weren't an easy thing.

"Chris . . . ?"

"I am fine, my friend."

I shucked the cylinder out of my Army and slipped another in. I could do the change without lookin', so I kept my eyes busy watchin' for more trouble. There weren't any. Fact, there wasn't no one nowhere.

"Cover my back, Chris." I said. "I want to look these skunks over. I got no idea why they braced me."

"They were paid," Chris replied. "The man I killed is a gun for hire, a bandit, and a horse thief. He spent most of his time in the bars in Taos and Santa Fe insulting innocent *señoritas*."

For the first time since Chris had showed up, I looked at him. He'd thinned down a little since the cabin fight, and it made his face sharp. He had a hard set to his mouth, and I reckoned this might be one mean Mexican if'n you insulted one of his sisters. The Mexican folks set store by their families, near as much as we Irish, and they usually settled such an insult with knives or guns.

I walked over to the dead men and quickly checked their shirt pockets. They were all carryin' newly minted gold money, one hundred and fifty dollars all told. It looked like Chris might be right. A hundred and fifty dollars was way more money than most men made in six months of hard work. It was money that we sorely needed at the ranch, but the truth was I felt a little funny 'bout keepin' it. I hadn't earned it, and I'd taken it off'n somebody else, even though I didn't figure they'd protest much.

The sutler had come out of the store, and I gave him twenty dollars of the gold.

"Better have somebody get them under the ground," I said "They smell bad enough already."

"That was the greatest thing I have ever seen, O'Malley. It was a fair shooting. I watched it all right from the store."

I sighed and wondered how he'd seen it all when he'd probably been layin' down on the floor behind the counter. I walked away from him, but I could feel his eyes on my back. His busy mouth tellin' a big story 'bout me was the last thing I needed, but I didn't figure there was any help for it. Chris followed me over to my horses.

"I heard the Major is gone," he said simply.

I nodded my head, but didn't turn to look at him. I was still havin' a case of the jitters, and my emotions were high.

"Did you come to the Garland for something, *señor*?" Chris asked me.

Chris was tryin' to find out what was goin' on without makin' it look like he was pushin'.

I looked at him and saw his face had gentled down. I also saw a man who had just backed me at risk of his own life. I knew that me and Chris Silva had just created a bond that would make us friends for the rest of our lives.

"I'm ridin' over to Denver," I said quiet. "I'd surely appreciate your company."

"I would be honored, *Señor* O'Malley. You are a man of my own heart. You are a man to ride with." I knew that was a high compliment comin' from a vaquero like Chris.

He turned and retrieved his horse from the south side of the fort. As he walked up to me, trailin' his horse behind, he looked at me with serious eyes. "You are a very fast man with the gun," he said. "I have never seen a thing like this before. You shot three times before I shot once."

"Someday I'll shoot too fast and kill the wrong man," I said, remembering the words of another friend back in Kansas.

"I don't believe so, *señor*. You are very fast, but you also think. It is important to think, even when your mind tells you to kill."

"I hope you're right," I said as I tightened my cinch. "I don't like the things I been hearin' 'bout myself. I don't want no more killin'."

Chris was quiet a moment as he adjusted the bit in his horse's mouth. He wiped his hand on a rag and looked over my way. "The man in the middle was Collin Rapage. He had the name of being a very bad man both among the Mexicans and the Anglos. It is said he has killed more than ten men. I have seen him fight before. He was very good with his pistol."

"He weren't good enough this time," I said, wantin' to change the subject.

"He wasn't even close, *amigo mío*," Chris said as he turned and tightened his own cinch.

I swung up onto my saddle and looked toward the main gate of the fort. There was some Army boys gatherin', and I didn't want to have to answer a bunch of fool questions. I had to get to Denver, but I had one thing left to do before I left.

"Wait on me, Chris. I'll be right back."

I rode through the gate, the Army men makin' a path for me, and stopped right in front of the door that said COMMANDANT over the top. I stepped off my horse, walked up the stairs, and opened the door. There was a major standin', lookin' from the window out across the dusty parade ground.

"I had myself a bit of a shootin' scrape out by the store," I explained. "Three men braced me and they come up dead. It was a fair shootin', and I reckon the sutler seen most of it. I got to get on over to Denver, but my brother, Captain Dan O'Malley, will speak for me. He'll tell ya that I ain't a bad sort of person." I took a deep breath and reached into my pocket. "I took this new gold money off'n them boys I shot. I don't feel right keepin' it even though I reckon it's blood to go there."

I was out of breath and not wantin' to carry on much of a conversation, so I dropped the gold on his desk, turned on my heel, and walked out. The last look I had at him, his mouth was fallen open like the door on an old outhouse.

I rode out the gate, and Chris was sittin' on the other side waitin' with his hand on his gun. If'n I'd've called out, he'd've taken on all of the U.S. Army. He was the kind of man you surely wanted for a partner.

We rode out of the fort, and as we passed the gate, I noticed a man standin' to the outside on the north that was wearin' a vest made from the hide of a Holstein milk cow. I shook my head, figurin' that it took all kinds to make the world run. I knew one thing sure, you weren't never gonna see me wearin' no milk cow vest. It just wasn't seemly.

We hit the main road for Denver and set a good pace for the pass that went over the Sangre de Cristo Mountains on the east side of the big valley. I was sorely troubled by the thought that someone might have paid to have me killed. I naturally thought of Nate Kurlow, but he seemed more the kind to want to shoot me hisself. It might be in the back, but he'd want the revenge. Fact was, if the Kurlows were as feudal as Dan had said, he'd be livin' for the day he could get me in his sights. That's not even addin' in the fact that Macon Beck was surely lookin' to get even with me for killin' his brother. Now, I reckoned I had another enemy somewhere that wanted me dead bad enough to lay out a pretty big piece of change. It was serious enough knowin' I had two enemies what wanted me dead, leave alone another fella that had laid out new gold to have me killed. It was enough to make a body want to head for the high-up hills and just get away from everybody. It surely did.

Chapter Four

Denver City had growed some since I'd last come down from the hills. The streets was busy and most of the businesses seemed to have people in 'em. There was big new buildings, buggies and buckboards lined the streets, and it was noisy.

According to what I'd heard, Denver started as two towns laid out just across the creek from each other. Denver City and Auraria were founded in 1859, pretty much along the banks of narrow Cherry Creek where a smidgen of gold had been found in 1858. There'd been some pretty heated competition for the first few years between the two towns 'bout who was gonna end up bein' the big dog. It finally ended with Auraria and Denver City joinin' up and becomin' Denver.

A. O. McGrew, who had pushed all his worldly belongin's from east Kansas to Denver in a wheelbarrow, made up a little poem which, when printed in *The Rocky Mountain News*, became the official ditty of Denver.

Speculation is the fashion even at this early stage,
And corner lots and big hotels appear to be the rage.
The emigration's bound to come, and to greet them we
   will try,
Big pig, little pig, root, hog, or die.

For all the big plans, the two towns still near died out that first year. The word spread back east about the great gold strike along the banks of Cherry Creek. As soon as the first breath of spring come on, folks started headin' for Cherry Creek. It proved to be a long, hard, and barren trip for most of 'em. Many of the movers died of starvation on the way west. Them that made the trip stayed a short while until they found out there weren't no gold, then headed back to the farms and towns of the East that they'd left behind. By April of '59, the gold rush was bein' called a giant hoax by all the papers in the East.

Then in May it happened. A near starved-out prospector hit a big strike of placer gold along the banks of Clear Creek some thirty miles west of Denver. Them that had been headin' back east turned around again and made the distance to the new find. Durin' the summer of '59 Denver's future was fixed as more and more strikes were made to the west of the town.

There'd been talk of the railroad comin' right through the center of town as early as 1862, but the engineer of the Union Pacific, General Dodge, reckoned that Berthoud Pass was too steep to push a rail grade over, and the Union Pacific went through Bridger's Pass a hundred miles to the north of Denver. There was Denver folks who said that the railroad missin' their town was the last stroke of God's hand, and Denver was soon to be ''too dead to bury.''

Byers, the owner of the loud and opinion-filled newspaper, *The Rocky Mountain News*, and other Denver business owners didn't believe Denver was dead, and soon set about building their own railroad north to the U.P. main line at Cheyenne.

We'd heard talk of the railway clear over to Saguache. It weren't done quite yet, but it was gettin' close, and the Denver boys was right proud of their railroad. It was also said that they was makin' a ton of money from the government, the Union Pacific, and stockholders in the company they'd formed. Besides the Denver company, the Kansas Pacific had reckoned that Denver would be a good place to include in their rail empire, and they was layin' track in from the east.

As Chris and me rode into town, the streets was crowded with miners, gamblers, drifters, cowboys, and painted women. It started out a wild place and hadn't toned down much in the nearly ten years it'd been settled. There was over forty saloons serving the five thousand souls that claimed to be residents, and the cemetery was home to over seven hundred folks that hadn't lived through the growin' pains of the first decade. It was a burg full of malcontents, most of 'em lookin' for a way to make a quick buck, or else they was people what run away from debt, marriages, or the law back East.

They weren't all bad. There was some folks in Denver, like the newspaper man Byers, that had a sense of what it took to make a town work. Some of the things they was doin' was takin' hold. The streets was wide and straight, somebody'd planted trees down both sides of most of 'em, and they even watered things durin' the summer to keep the dust down. It felt like Denver was a town gettin' ready to pop and become a city. Too many people, too much noise, and the buildin's was crammed in too small a space for my taste.

We rode straight to the pine-board eatin' house on one of the side streets. We'd called the eatin' house The Rainbow City after the same kinda place we'd had in Kansas.

We tied the horses up to the rail and tried to brush some of the dust off 'fore we went in. We was dirty, hungry, and thirsty after the ride, and I could smell the food bein' cooked inside. My mouth started slaverin' like a coyote standin' over a dead possum.

As we walked in, I seen Lee. She didn't notice us for a minute, and I had a chance to look at her. She was a mite skinny 'cept she was filled out pretty well in them places where a gal ought to be. I still remembered the first time I'd seen her. She'd been layin' under a dead man on a stage coach that'd been attacked. I'd been some surprised by her spunk. She was packin' a pistol, and she knew how to use it. She wasn't comin' all to pieces like most women. I reckoned there weren't many women would've done what she did.

She was a downright purty girl, and it still struck me that I was one lucky man that this girl had seen fit to take a likin' to me.

"Matt," she said kinda excited-like when she seen me standin' in the door. She come runnin' over and got hold of me 'round the neck. She actually kissed me right full on the mouth, and I felt the color come up in my face.

"Lee, doggone it, people are lookin'."

"I'm sorry, Matt, but it's been so darn long. . . ."

"It's been too long," I agreed. "I got caught up in the ranch work and all the things happenin' 'round there. . . ." My voice trailed off as I remembered what we was doin' here.

"Matthew, what's wrong?"

I never been much good at hidin' things from people. "Chris, you want to order up a bait of food whilst Lee and me go into the back room for a minute?" I asked my partner.

Chris nodded and wandered over to a table near the front windows. "Let's go into the back, Lee," I said quiet, steerin' her through the maze of tables.

When I told her about the cabin fight and the Major, she cried some, stopped for a spell, and then started all over again. The Major had been like a father to Lee, and she took losin' him right hard.

"I'll be fine, Matt," she said after a while. She looked up at me with wet, red eyes. "Why don't you go out and get some food. I'll wash my face and come out in a few minutes."

I nodded, feelin' some relief. I'd never been no 'count with cryin' women. I walked back into the main dinin' room and over to Chris.

"Do not look my friend, but I think we may have someone watching us." Chris busied himself rollin' a cigarette, and then spoke again.

"It is the man across the street wearing the Holstein vest. Not many men would wear a vest such as that. He was at the fort, and I noticed him as we entered the edge of town. Now he is standing across the street. I do not think this thing is coincidence."

"Does look like maybe we was expected," I agreed, gazing at the vest man while appearing to talk to Chris.

Chris was right. Not many men would wear a vest that'd been made out of a Holstein milk critter.

"I'll have a piece of meat and some spuds," I said to the girl that was servin' as she walked by. She nodded, smiled at me, and went toward the kitchen.

Lee come from the back room and sat down at the table with

us. "I got a new cook that I put on a few days ago," she said. "He's near as good as the Major was when it comes to bakin'." Her bottom lip trembled a little, but she took hold and didn't cry. "He baked up some dry apple pies today, and yesterday he baked bread. I'm thinkin' he'll be bringing some extra business in."

We talked for a spell about the cattle and what the partnership had planned for the ranch. We went over what we figured this winter up in the high meadows was gonna be like, and if the partnership was gonna survive the two years it was gonna take to recover from our winter losses. After a while Lee hit right on what I'd been steppin' around.

"What does the partnership want to do with Rainbow City?" she asked.

I looked at her purty face and had a powerful hope she'd want to sell the place off to somebody else. I wanted her to come out to the ranch 'fore winter, and the money we'd realize from the sale would tide us over for a good part of the winter.

"When we talked, they decided to let you make the call on the place," I replied. "They said you could either keep on runnin' it or sell it, whichever you wanted."

She was quiet a minute, lookin' out onto the street through the window. "I'll think 'bout it," she said, "but I'd kinda like to come out to the ranch. I do all right here, but I'm a farm girl. I don't hold with all these people crammed together."

"I know that feelin'," I agreed.

Far as I knew, Lee didn't have no family nowheres. I knew both of her parents was dead, and I didn't think there was anyone else. The O'Malley clan was as much family as she had left, and it'd been in the back of my mind to make her a real part of the O'Malley family. Trouble was, I weren't no good at such things. I was a fair hand with a gun, passable with a rope and brandin' iron, and I could even read and do ciphers. I wasn't worth shucks when it come to girls.

"Did you know that Ara Turbeck is starring at the opera house?" Lee asked, changin' the subject.

"Nope. Hadn't heard that," I replied, thinking about the dark-haired, pretty Irish girl I'd first met on the plains of Kansas. I knew she'd gotten into singin' and play-actin' after we'd moved to the territory, but I didn't know she was travelin' 'round doin' it.

"She's gotten famous, or so one of my table girls told me. She's sung for governors in three states and is 'sposed to be headin' for Washington to sing for the President."

"Do tell," I said, tryin' not to act too interested. Me and Ara Turbeck kinda had a thing goin' back in the grasslands, and Lee knew 'bout it. Fact was, for a spell I'd fancied myself in love with Ara. We were never nothin' serious, particular after she saw me have a shootin' scrape with some scum that was tryin' to kill my brother Owen. I was purty dumb when it come to girls, but I had learned that women are notional, kinda like Injuns. I didn't want trouble with Lee, and I reckoned the best way to stay out of trouble about Ara was to keep my mouth shut.

My slab of meat come, and I got right busy makin' it disappear down my craw. I was hopin' by the time I got done eatin' Lee might've forgot about Ara.

I heard the door close and looked up to see a man walkin' across the room. He was wearin' a black suit with a string tie and white shirt, and I pegged him for a gambler or maybe a saloon owner. He had brilliant white hair cut close and a magnificent black mustache under his nose. I'd never seen a man with white hair and black mustache before, and it surely made a body take a second look. He was a big man with large hands, wide shoulders, and pale blue eyes. He had a square jaw and a small cleft in his chin. I realized that in some quarters he might be considered a downright handsome man. The problem was, he looked mighty familiar to me. It was like I'd knowed him a long time ago in a place far away. I shrugged and looked back down to my plate.

"Now there is another man talking with the vest man," Chris said in a hushed tone.

I looked out the window and saw that another man had joined the greenhorn in the Holstein vest. The new guy was wearin' a dude suit and had a bowler on his head. Now, I reckoned a man had a right to wear whatever kinda hat he wanted. It was a free country after all. I also figured that a man with guts enough to wear a bowler in cow country had to be either really stupid or a hard man. Both Holstein and Bowler had the look of folks just lately in from the East, but neither of them looked soft. They just looked new.

All of a sudden, I was tired of it. I was downright sick of being follered, watchin' over my shoulder all the time, and waitin' for a bullet to come out of the dark. What really made me mad was that them boys across the street was spoilin' my meal. I was a feller what set store by good food, and I surely hated bein' upset whilst I was tryin' to eat. I scooted my chair back, dropped my fork beside my plate, and headed for the door.

"Matt," Lee called after me.

"Stay put. I'll be right back," I said over my shoulder, meaning it for both Chris and Lee.

I strode right across the street and stopped dead in front of Mr. Holstein.

"If I'd a notion that you was follerin' me 'round the country, I'd surely be gettin' mad 'bout now," I said in an even voice. I was icy cold and calm. I'd been in some fights both with guns and fists, and I reckoned I could handle myself.

Mr. Holstein looked a mite uncomfortable, and Mr. Bowler Hat started edgin' around to my left side. I stopped him with a gesture.

"You keep movin', and I'm gonna blow you right out from under that funny-lookin' hat," I said in a conversational tone. He stopped movin' and started sweatin'.

"You got an answer for me?" I asked Mr. Holstein.

"He works for me, Matthew," a deep voice said from behind me.

Well, now I'd went and done it. I could almost hear Kiowa's voice and Wedge's too. They'd told me time and again never to underestimate the people I was goin' against, and here I was boxed neater than a store-bought pie.

If these boys was part and parcel of the ones tryin' to kill me, I was in serious trouble. I reckoned I knew what I was gonna do next, but I'd no idea what they was. I didn't see guns on either of the men to my front, but they didn't seem particular concerned neither.

"We are not a threat to you, Matthew," the voice behind me said again. Then it struck me, the man behind me was callin' me by my given name.

"I reckon we got us a problem here," I said. "You seem to know me, but if I turn to look at you, these two coyotes are gonna jump me. I got a notion to shoot both of them, and then turn and look at you."

"I mean it, Matt. We mean you no harm."

"I am here, *amigo mío,*" Chris said simply. His voice came from behind and one side of me.

"You wanta watch these two boys while I talk to the gent behind me?" I asked.

"Certainly," Chris replied.

I turned and looked. It was the white-haired man from the eatin' house, and he had a big smile on his face.

"You have the look of your father." His voice was deep, and his speech was not the careless talk of back-country. He knew me, and he knew Pa, but I'd be hanged if I could place him.

"Both of these men work for me, and they have been following you since Fort Garland," he said. "They telegraphed me your location, and I asked them to tag along behind you until I could get here from Bent's Fort. I just rode in this morning."

"Why would you be lookin' for me?" I asked, curious why such a man would have an interest in someone like me. He was obviously a man of education, and I reckoned he traveled in circles that I wouldn't be comfortable in.

"I was not only looking for you, but for all of your family. I've come a long way." He reached up and touched the corner of his mustache with his forefinger, then continued. "The last I heard, your mother and father had settled in Pennsylvania and were farming. I was surprised that your father could settle down long enough to raise a crop."

I started to say somethin' 'bout him layin' off that kinda talk 'bout Pa, but he held up his hand to quiet me.

"I found the farm, your mother's grave, and the neighbors told me about you coming west. I heard stories about you and the rest of the family in Kansas. You have a lot of friends back there, and folks enjoyed talking about the O'Malley brothers. Mostly the talk was about you. The young O'Malley.''

I started to say somethin', and again he stopped me.

''I lost your trail at Bent's Fort a few weeks ago and sent William and Tommy ahead to see if they could find a trace of where you'd gone. I'd heard rumors there were a clan of O'Malley's in the mountains, but couldn't find any information of substance.'' He took a step toward me and put his hand in his pocket. ''Then you had the little problem at Fort Garland. William saw the fight and heard the sutler call you by name. That's when they telegraphed me.''

''Why all this interest in the O'Malleys, and who the heck are you?'' I asked.

''My name is John O'Malley,'' he said in that deep voice of his. ''I'm brother to your father. I'm your uncle.''

I sucked in a little wind, took a step back, and looked close at him. No wonder he looked familiar. He was bigger than Pa, and maybe a mite better lookin', but I could see the resemblance. I'd heard tell that there was some other O'Malleys around, but I'd never given it much thought.

He looked past me at the two men behind me. ''Tommy, you and William gather up the rest of the men. I arranged for rooms at a boardinghouse around the corner.'' He pointed off toward the north, and the two men moved to follow his orders. He looked back at me. ''Let's go back to the restaurant, and I'll catch you up.''

''*Señor,* I have business . . .''

''Go ahead, Chris. I'll be at The Rainbow City when you get done,'' I said to Silva.

''A good man,'' Uncle John said as he watched Chris walk away. ''The O'Malleys have always had good men around them.''

We walked back to The Rainbow City and sat down again near the window. I weren't near as hungry as I had been, but Lee come from the kitchen carryin' a whole dried apple pie, and me and Uncle John talked as we worked our way through it.

"Your father is the oldest of ten. There were six brothers and four sisters, but two of the girls died when they were still children. Tirley was indentured to a silversmith when he was eight, and his small earnings helped support the family. When he turned twelve, there was an incident with the silversmith, and he left New York. He came West. The edge of the frontier in those days was still Missouri, and that's where he joined his first fur brigade. Tirley was always a wild one." Uncle John was lookin' from the window, but he was seein' farther that just down the street.

"We got a couple of letters from him, and he came back to the city once, but the wild land had claimed him. During that first visit home, he tore up three or four bars and cut up a tough with a knife bigger than most swords. He left again, and we didn't hear from him for nearly twenty years. We finally got a letter that said he'd married and settled down on a farm. I couldn't see that life for him, but he must've made a go of it."

"He spent a fair 'mount of time huntin' and trekkin'," I said, remembering the restlessness that always seemed to lie just under Pa's skin.

"He'd seen the elephant, or so he told me on that visit home," John remarked. "Tirley said once you see the elephant there's nothing quite like it, and you have to see more. I didn't know quite what he was talking about, but I knew the wild country was what he loved and longed for."

"Seein' the elephant is an old mountain man sayin'," I told John. "It meant that they'd crossed the rivers and seen many a mountaintop. From the stories he told us boys, he'd surely seen the elephant."

We fell quiet and looked at each other over the empty pie tin. "Have you heard any word of him, Matthew?" Uncle John finally asked me.

I shook my head and looked down at my hands. "Last I seen him he was hikin' down the road goin' toward the war."

"Sounds like him," Uncle John said.

"I just don't feel like he's dead, but surely he'd have tried to find us if he was still alive," I said.

"Unless he wasn't able to. A lot of things happened during the war. There are men still looking for their families that were displaced during the fighting. There are a lot of families waiting for their soldiers to come home."

"Most of 'em ain't comin' home now," I observed. "There's been time enough."

John nodded his head and looked down the street. "Here comes your partner," he said, seein' Chris walking toward us, "and I need to make sure my men are settled in." He was quiet a minute and then looked back to me. "Would you and your friend like to come to the opera house with me tonight? I have tickets to the performance."

I thought of what Lee had told me about Ara and hesitated. I looked over at Lee cleanin' tables and askin' folks 'bout their meal. She'd be workin' late at The Rainbow City, so I reckoned it wouldn't hurt to just take a peek at the show.

"Sure, we'd be right honored to go with ya," I replied.

"I will meet you in front of the opera house at seven forty-five," John said. "The show starts at eight."

I nodded my head, and Uncle John scooted back his chair. He smiled at me and left. Chris come walkin' in and sat down where John had been sittin'. We were lookin' out the window when I seen a carriage drive by. It weren't a buggy or a surrey. It was a full-blown carriage like the rich folks have back in the big cities. I caught a glimpse of a man lookin' from one of the windows, and then it was gone on down the street. I took notice of it 'cause it was the first coach I'd seen in a spell. They just weren't that common.

"Your uncle has enemies," Chris said as soon as he'd settled in. "The man in the carriage is one of them."

"What are ya talkin' about?" I asked curiously.

"John O'Malley is a man of influence in a big city in the East, amigo. Now, he has decided to come west. He is an owner of railroads. My people know little more than this, but it is said that he has enemies that will kill him if they can." He stopped a minute and looked down the street after the carriage. ''The man's name is Daniel Briggs. It is said that he has made a fortune on the railroads, and he is now looking for ground. A lot of ground, *señor.*''

''He one of them speculators then?'' I asked.

''He is that and more. He is rich, powerful, and knows the governor of this land personally. It is also said that he hates your uncle with all of his heart, but there is more than just this. It is said that he hates all of the O'Malleys. It is something to do with an O'Malley that made him lose face with a general during the war.''

''How do you find these things out?'' I asked.

''People talk around their servants like they are not there. There are many Mexican people who are servants in this town. They talk among themselves about the strange actions of the Anglos. I am known to them, and they talk to me if I ask, *señor.*''

What Chris said made good sense to me. I knew many of the white folks had help, and most of the servants were Mexicans in this part of the country. They worked cheap, did most anything they was asked, and kept their mouths shut. I also knew that many of the servants was treated purty poor and were figured to be no 'count. Most whites put the Mexicans right there on the social ladder with the Injuns and the blacks. It weren't right, but that's the way it was.

''I also found out that your uncle is a very dangerous man,'' Chris added.

''Well, we know he's got men hired 'cause of Cow Vest and Bowler, and it sounded like he had others besides them two.''

''No, Matthew. Your Uncle is a very dangerous man himself. He is said to have killed a man recently in a duel, and he also fights with his hands.'' Chris looked a little disgusted, and I knew that most Mexicans couldn't see the need of abusin' your hands when a knife worked so much better. I was a peaceable man by nature, but I was still kinda partial to fist-fightin' myself.

''What are you tryin' to say, Chris?'' He had something stuck in his craw, and I wanted him to spit it out.

''Someone hired three men to kill you. They paid in new gold coin. Your uncle is a rich man. Could he lose something to you and your brothers? Is there something you do not know about your family in the East? Perhaps there was a family treasure that you should legally share in,'' Chris smiled that darn smile of his where all of his teeth showed under his mustache.

''You got it wrong. Uncle John ain't that kinda man. He holds store by his family.''

''What do you know of your uncle?'' Chris was quiet a minute, lettin' that sink in. ''You know only what he has told you.''

I blew air out of my nose and shook my head. What Chris was tellin' me was contrary to everything I knew about the O'Malleys. Pa'd told me time and again that our clan was downright fetched in the head when it come to defendin' our family. The O'Malleys had always been that way.

''I am not saying what I have told you is true, but it is a thing to think about. You do not even know if he is really your uncle.''

Chris was right, and it kinda stirred me some. I guessed I was so trustin' that I just took people for what they said. I had to admit to myself that I was still young and had a lot of learnin' to do. I just weren't used to people lyin', but I knew they did.

''He may be your uncle, and what he says may be all true, but you must go with caution. Hold a portion of your mind aside and watch. If he is lying, it will be shown.''

I looked sharply at Chris. The things he'd told me made more sense than I cared to admit, but where'd he learn all that stuff? He weren't much older than me, and I figured he'd never been away from the San Luis Haciendas before he'd come over to the Storm King. I didn't know much 'bout John O'Malley, but it occurred to me that I didn't know much 'bout Chris Silva neither.

''It looks like I'm gonna be late gettin' out tonight, Matt.'' Lee's voice broke through my thoughts, and I looked up.

''We're gonna bed down over at the livery,'' I replied. ''Why don't you go ahead on to bed when you close, and we'll come over in the mornin'. We can talk some and maybe decide where we're headin'.''

She put her hand on my shoulder and smiled. ''I know where I want to go, Matt.''

I gulped and swallered big. I felt like a mangy skunk for not tellin' her I was goin' to the opera house.

She squeezed my shoulder and walked away quick to help some folks find a seat. It was near suppertime, and the place was fillin' up.

"Let's go get cleaned up," I said to Chris.

He was grinnin' like a 'possum eatin' watermelon. I near shot him right on the spot.

Chapter Five

Her voice was as clear as a mountain lake, and the song was as Irish as the green land itself. I could scarce believe that this was the same person I'd known on the plains of Kansas. When I'd last seen her, Ara had still been a girl. Now she was a woman growed, and beautiful at that. It was no wonder that the theaters and opera houses filled to standin' room only when she showed up.

"She's wonderful, isn't she?" Uncle John asked as people clapped for her when she'd finished singin'.

"She's always had a purty voice," I replied, remembering the good times when she'd come to our cabin in Junction City. That was when she still liked me. Owen and Wedge had been quite an item with their singin' back there, and sometimes Ara had joined in their songs.

"You mean to tell me you know this lady?" Uncle John asked me in a tone that made my back hair come up.

"We was friends in Kansas," I said shortly.

John left it lay, and Chris stirred in the seat on the other side of me.

"We should leave, *señor,*" he whispered. "There are too many people, and they are too close together. If we leave in a crowd, it would be a simple matter to stick a knife in you."

I'd listened to Ara sing with the rest of the crowd for nearly an hour. She'd captured us all, and nary a word was spoken the whole time she sang. Now, some idiot with his face painted black was on the stage actin' out somethin' that I couldn't get a handle on.

"Uncle John, me and Chris are goin' outside to catch some air," I whispered.

John nodded, but didn't let his attention leave the idiot on the stage. We got up and walked down the center aisle of the opera house to the door in the back. The night air smelled of horse apples, cigar smoke, and faintly of pine trees. It was cool outside, and I was glad we'd left.

The streets was lit by several pitch-dipped torches stuck in holders, and the uncertain light made the shadows dance along the boardwalks. The shadows brought to my mind the stories of banshees and other night things, and I had an uneasy feelin'.

"What are your plans, my friend?" Chris asked me as he leaned against the building and built a smoke.

"I'm gonna try and work up the courage to ask Lee if she'll marry me," I said bluntly. "If she'll have me, we'll load her stuff, rent a buckboard, turn The Rainbow City over to the new cook, and head back for the ranch. We'll have Otto Mears marry us in Saguache when we get back."

It was the first time I'd put my thoughts into words, but I knew that a family and life with Lee was what I wanted. I'd made up my mind whilst I'd been listenin' to Ara sing an Irish love ballad.

"That is good. You and she fit well together. You will have a good life," Chris remarked.

I heard a door close on the side of the opera house. We was standin' right at the mouth of a side street, and when I looked toward the door, I sucked in a little wind. Ara had stepped out into the cool night air not twenty feet from us, and she was lookin' right at me.

"How are you, Matthew?"

Now, I'm not given to stutter and stammer, but she'd taken me by surprise.

"I . . . I . . . I reckon I'm purty fair," I managed.

"I thought I saw you come in, and then I was sure I saw you leave. Did you enjoy my songs?"

"It was the best thing I've heard since you last sung with the boys back in Kansas," I said.

She nodded and moved closer to me. "I miss those times,

Matthew,'' she said, raising her delicate hand to her face. ''Life was simple then. We were children without complications or responsibilities.'' Her voice sounded right soulful, and I felt my heart jump just a mite.

''Kansas was good to us, at least for a spell,'' I said. ''Then things kinda got confused.'' I looked around to see where Chris was and saw he was walkin' away across the street. It looked like he was gonna leave me here talkin' to a girl. I'd a rather fought a 'Pache brave bare-handed than try and carry on talkin' with a woman such as Ara had become.

''How are the rest of the clan?'' Ara asked.

''The Major was killed in a fight with renegades, and Owen was hurt powerful bad. The rest of us are doin' good, and we got us a nice ranch over in the San Luis Valley.''

''I knew about the ranch,'' Ara said. ''I saw Lee when we first arrived in Denver.'' Ara looked off down the street and then back up into my face. ''Lee told me she wants to marry you and move out to the ranch.''

I swallered big and nodded my head. ''It ain't gonna be easy for me, but I'm gonna ask her in the mornin'.''

''She's suited to you, Matthew, and you to her. I'm sure you will have a wonderful and happy life,'' she said. I thought I could see some tears buildin' in Ara's eyes, but the light weren't good, and I couldn't tell for sure.

Men started comin' in ones and twos from the opera house, signaling that the show was almost over.

''I wish things had turned out differently for us, Matthew,'' Ara said in a quiet, sweet voice. She took a few steps closer until she was near right against me. ''There was a time when I really did love you.'' She hesitated a minute and looked deep into my eyes. ''Perhaps I still do, a little.''

I felt my ears gettin' hot, and I didn't know what to say. Ara stood on her tiptoes, wrapped her arms around my neck, and kissed me full on the mouth. It weren't one of those sister kisses like sometimes a gal will lay on ya. No sir, this here was a feelin' kiss 'cause I felt it all the way down to my toes.

I figured I ought to be fightin' her off, but my knees was so

weak I couldn't have fought off a gnat. Instead, my arms kinda
went 'round her natural. I reckoned I was tryin' to hold myself
up. She held on for so long I thought I was gonna pass out for
lack of breathin', and then she stepped back. There was tears on
her cheeks, but a tiny smile rested on her lips. The men 'round
us was clappin', and I turned to glare at 'em. They moved off
with some quiet laughs.

"Stay well, Matthew, and take good care of Lee."

"I'll do my level best."

Ara turned and entered the door on the side of the building.
She was gone, but the memory of her kiss was still on my lips.
I looked to see if Chris had been watchin'. All I needed was that
darn Mexican givin' me a hard time about bein' a lover.

Instead of Chris, I spotted Lee standin' 'bout halfway across
the street. The light of the torches showed her face. She had her
hand to her mouth, and she looked like she'd been bit by a big
rattler.

"Lee . . ." I started toward her to try and explain, but she
turned and ran back toward The Rainbow City. "Lee . . ." I
called out after her.

There was more men comin' from the opera house, and the
street was gettin' busy with folks walkin' home. I started walkin'
the direction she'd taken, feelin' like a gut-shot, mangy, flea-bit
coyote. I wouldn't have hurt Lee for nothin', but the innocent
good-bye she'd seen between me and Ara had to look purty bad.
Fact, if the spots was switched, and I'd seen Lee kissin' some
man like Ara kissed me, I'd've been up on my horse and headin'
for the high-up hills.

Suddenly, I heard loud voices comin' from an alley.

"We gonna show you what we do to uppity greasers in this
town," a loud, coarse voice said.

I pulled even with the mouth of the alley and looked in. There
was soft yellow light spillin' from the windows of the stores on
both sides. I could plainly see four men facing down my partner,
Chris Silva. It looked as if they meant to give him a beatin'.

"Why don't you boys go find some other poor fella to beat

on,'' I said in a conversational tone as I walked into the alley. I felt the old burnin' start down in my gut.

A big man with a full beard and long greasy hair tuned on me. He looked at me a moment and then gave a nasty grin.

''You'd best get back to your mommy, boy. This here's man's business, and you could get hurt.''

''Well, I got this little problem, mister,'' I replied in an even tone. ''That there Mexican is my friend. In fact, he's my saddle partner. I stand with him no matter what comes.''

''Well, that means you're gonna get a piece of what we had saved for him,'' the man said with a snarl.

There weren't no guns out, so I reckoned it was somethin' that would have to be done with fists.

All of a sudden I felt good. I wasn't a man to go huntin' a fight, but, on the other hand, I'd never stepped aside from fightin'. I could feel the old rage startin' to come over me. It was the killin' storm that took me now and again, and it scared me.

One of the big man's friends turned toward me while the other two started toward Chris.

''Jack, you might be taking on a bit more than you bargained for,'' Uncle John's deep voice said from behind me. Seemed lately he was always behind me just when a fight was commencin'.

The big man stopped comin' for a minute and looked past me.

''You got no cause to mix in this, O'Malley. It's got nothin' to do with you.''

''I'm sorry, Jack, but it does. The man you're facing is my nephew, Matthew O'Malley, late of Kansas. I think you've heard his name before. The other man is Christian Silva.''

''Not the Taos Silva?'' one of the toughs asked.

''It is,'' Uncle John confirmed. I had no idea what they was talkin' about, but it seemed to have an effect on 'em.

''I expect I wouldn't really need to help my nephew and his friend, but I have a bad habit of mixing myself in O'Malley trouble.''

The air felt heavy with tension, and I could hear the breathin' of the men that stood in front of me. It was touch and go there for a minute, but finally the big man looked back over his shoulder at his other two men.

"The time ain't right, boys. Back off," the man named Jack said.

They all stepped to the other side of the alley and walked out onto the street, muttering among themselves.

"That was Jack Fallon," John explained as Chris and I stepped out of the alley. "He likes to call himself Black Jack, but he doesn't amount to much. He always has to have a gang to back his play. We've known each other for quite a while, and we're always on opposite sides of the issues."

"Thank you, *señor*. They would have beaten me badly had you and Matthew not helped me," Chris said to John.

John smiled at Chris and then bit the end off a long black cigar. "You might have handled them, Silva."

"Perhaps, but it would have been painful for all involved, and I would have surely killed at least one of them." I saw the gleam of naked steel as Chris leaned down and slipped a nasty-looking, slim-bladed knife into the top seam of his boot. "It is bad for a Mexican to kill a white man in a white man's town," Chris observed. "The Mexican will never be right no matter what the odds or cause."

"You are correct, of course," John agreed.

"What'd ya mean when you told 'em about Chris and Taos?" I asked. "It seemed to slow 'em down some."

"You haven't told him?" John asked Chris.

"No, *señor*. It was only a small thing."

"You should have told him," John said quietly.

Chris shook his head, looked at me, then back to Uncle John.

"Matthew called me his friend this night. It is the first time I have ever had a friend. Would he be my friend if he knew about this small thing in New Mexico?" Chris took a breath and shrugged. "I do not think the O'Malley brothers would have hired me had they known about Taos, and I would not have this friend."

"Don't sell the O'Malleys short, Christian. Matthew has had his share of trouble, and men have died by his hand, as you know.

What you did in Taos was in the name of law and order, and it was a thing that needed to be done.''

''What the heck are you two talkin' about?'' I asked, finally gettin' in a word.

''Christian Silva has something of a reputation with both a gun and a knife,'' Uncle John explained. ''He is also known to be extremely unforgiving.''

John put his back against the nearest building and began his story. ''It seems there was a rather large extended family made up of mostly of boys by the last name of Gonzales. They were a rough bunch and rode as a family of bandits with the grand-father as their leader. With cousins thrown in, the Gonzales family made up a gang of over a dozen men. They raided, stole horses, robbed stages and banks, and raped and pillaged on both sides of the border for nearly five years. One day last summer they came as far north as Taos, where they terrorized the town for several hours. They literally tore down a saloon, set fire to the mercantile, slapped a few women around, and were starting for the bank when a single man stepped out into the street in front of them. He'd been hired as the town marshal a few weeks before and felt he had a job to do. On top of that, his sister had been one of the women that had been beaten by the bandits.'' John stopped a minute, looked at one of the street torches, and continued. ''The marshal must have known when he stepped out onto the street that he was going to die, but it was a matter of pride with him. He had a job to do, and the honor of his family was at stake.''

Uncle John stopped speaking, pulled the torch from the holder, and lit his cigar. When he had it smokin' like an old steam en-gine, he replaced the torch, stepped back onto the boardwalk, and blew a smoke ring out toward the night sky.

''Well . . . ?'' I said, wanting him to finish the story.

''When the smoke cleared, the marshal was still standing and seven of the gang were lying dead on the street. Six of them were shot, and one of them had a peculiar, narrow-blade knife sticking from his throat. The distance was probably fifty feet, so the knife had to have been thrown as accurately as if it had been shot from a pistol. Among the dead were the two oldest sons of old man Gonzales and Gonzales himself. The rest of the gang ran.''

Uncle John took a puff from his cigar, blew another smoke ring, watching it with satisfaction, and looked over at me.

''The marshal took up the chase and killed two more in a running battle with the gang on the way south toward Santa Fe. He caught up with the rest of the outlaws just north of Santa Fe when they decided to fort up at a spring. That's where they died.''

''The marshal's name . . . ?'' I asked, knowin' the answer.

''Christian Silva,'' John said quietly. ''Your friend.''

''There was one left, *señor*,'' Chris said, correcting Uncle John.

''You took care of him at Fort Garland,'' I said, remembering what he'd told me before the shootin' started.

''I did,'' Chris admitted.

''That's why the men that had him treed here in the alley turned a little white around the edges when I mentioned his name,'' John said. ''They might have tried you alone, Matthew, and they might have tried Chris alone, but they weren't going to take both of you, and they knew it.'' John took a puff from the cigar again. I thought the cigar smelled something like burnin' buffalo chips, but he seemed to enjoy it. ''You have acquired a sizable reputation yourself, Matthew.''

''It's not a thing I've sought after,'' I remarked.

John nodded and looked down the street toward The Rainbow City. ''I could use another piece of that excellent pie,'' he remarked.

''I need to get up there anyhow,'' I said. ''I got to talk to Lee.''

Just as I finished speaking, the hollow boom of a big rifle sounded from across the street. Uncle John fell to the boardwalk, and I had my Colt out, lettin' it rip and snort. I could hear other shots as I started walkin' toward the dark alley across the street. With my last shot I saw a Winchester fall into the uncertain light of the torches, and then a man fell on top of it. I switched cylinders and ran soft-footed to the protection of a store that bordered the dark lane, expecting a shot at any moment. I grabbed a torch and held it so the alley was lit up.

"There is no one else, my friend," Chris said from the storefront on the other side.

I tossed the torch to Chris, and he began checking the man we'd shot. I ran back across the street as men began to gather on the boardwalks. Shots at night were not an uncommon thing in Denver, but shots that sounded like a war was goin' were sure to attract some attention.

"I'm fine, Matthew. The bullet cut across my back. It hurts, but it's not too bad." John had his jacket and shirt off, and Cow Vest was tendin' to him.

"For me or you?" I asked, thinking about the shot from the dark.

"I think that one was for me," he replied. "I seemed to have made some enemies the past few years."

"I know the feelin'," I said sympathetically.

"Matt, would you be for helpin' me get him to his room?" Cow Vest asked.

"Sure," I said lookin' at him. "Which one are you, anyhow?"

"I'm Tommy O'Neal," the man answered in a tenor voice with a heavy Irish brogue and then gave me a big smile. "I know what you think of me clothes, laddie, but I'm just stubborn enough to not want to change them."

"It ain't all your clothes, it's that vest. It just ain't seemly for a man to wear a piece of a milk cow critter."

"The leather for me vest came over on the boat with me. It's from our old milk cow that saved me family's life during a time of starvation. I plan to keep it, I do."

"Well, Tommy O'Neal, I'd best teach you how to use a shotgun 'cause sure 'nuff some liquored-up cowhand is gonna try and peel it off ya."

"They may come when they will. I will show them a thing or two about we Irish lads."

I helped O'Neal get Uncle John on his feet and turned as Chris came walkin' up behind us.

"Matt, it is a rifle like the one you took at the cabin fight."

Chris handed me the Winchester, and I looked it over. It was a brother to the one I'd left back at the ranch.

"He also had this in his pocket." Chris laid some brand-new gold money in my hand, and I squeezed my fist around it. Looked like Uncle John and I had some of the same enemies.

We walked John to the roomin' house, and Tommy O'Neal started cleanin' the wound with some mighty powerful bottle alcohol. I knew it hurt by the way Uncle John's jaw bunched up, but he said nary a word.

"I'm goin' over to the eatin' house," I said, and turned to leave. I stopped a moment and turned back toward John. "I'll come get you in the mornin' for breakfast, and we'll talk. I still don't know how come you been lookin' for me and my brothers, but I'd bet there's more to it than just brotherly love."

The Rainbow City was dark by the time we got there. I was still feelin' mighty poorly about what had happened with Lee, but it weren't right for me to go knockin' on her door after the lights was out. I'd just have to wait and talk with her in the mornin'.

Chris and me got our bedrolls from our saddles in the livery, I patted Sin horse on the neck and hand-fed him some corn, then me and Chris rolled out on some sweet-smellin' grass hay.

Mornin' came 'fore I was ready. I never been one that lays in the blankets after my eyes fly open, but it'd been a late night, and I was still tired. I groaned as I stood up, and then stretched until my bones popped. Chris was already up and dressed. He was givin' the horses a bait of oats, and he'd throwed some hay in the stall mangers.

"Good morning, *amigo mío*," he said cheerful like. I walked past him without talkin' and shoved my head and shoulders into the horse trough to clear my brain. The water was cold, and I came up snortin' and blowin'. I combed out my hair and shaved off the little stubble of beard along my jaws and chin. By the time I got my hat on, I was feelin' near like I was gonna live.

"Matthew O'Malley?" a voice said off to the side of the barn.

My hand dropped to my gun, which was the first thing I always put on in the mornin', and slipped the keeper thong off the hammer. I turned and faced the man. The mornin' sun was shinin' in his face, which gave me an advantage.

"I'm O'Malley," I said shortly. I spotted the badge on his vest and relaxed a little. The law had no call for me that I knew of.

"My name is Deputy Sheriff Shadrach Taylor. Your Uncle says you were involved in a shooting last night."

I'd heard the name Shadrach before when Ma had taught us some of the teachin's from the Good Book. Seemed to me that there'd been a Shadrach, Meshach, and one other feller what I couldn't recall.

"There was some shootin'," I agreed, "and I reckon I was close about." I was really kinda wonderin' if Deputy Shadrach had any brothers, and if he did, I bet I knew what their names were.

"I've talked to enough witnesses that I know it was a fair shooting, Mr. O'Malley. I am more concerned with the rifle you picked up from the man who was killed."

"It's layin' back there by my saddle," I said, pointing into the livery.

Deputy Shadrach Taylor walked in through the open door and picked up the Winchester. He looked it over close, then laid it back down by my saddle.

"I can't be sure, but I suspect that rifle is one of those stolen from a rail car in Kansas City a few months ago. There was a shipment of over a hundred new Winchesters taken from the train right in broad daylight. Whoever did it planned well and had a place to go with them. We got a telegraph on it from Kansas City, and new Winchesters have been turning up out here in the hands of some very bad people."

"I got another one back at the ranch," I said. "Took it off'n a Ute renegade."

"That's what I mean. There's no way that rifle should have ended up with an Ute."

"You got any brothers?" I finally worked up the courage to ask.

He looked puzzled and then smiled. I knew in that moment Deputy Taylor and me was gonna be friends. "I have two brothers, Mr. O'Malley. I think my father and mother made sure there were at least three boys. I mean, really, without three of us, what would be the point? I am the oldest, my brother, Meshach is second, and my youngest brother's name is Abendigo. My father greatly admired the courage of those Old Testament heroes, and told us he wanted us to grow up to be just like them. I think we've tried since we're all lawmen of one kind or another.''

"I don't reckon many folks forget your name,'' I said with a smile.

"No, I rarely have to repeat it,'' Taylor said.

We walked back into the light of the mornin' and Deputy Shad looked at me.

"The man that was killed last night was a sure-thing killer from California. He showed up here about two weeks ago and has been hanging around with a rough string. Many of his associates are employees of Nathan Kurlow.''

I started at the name and looked hard at the deputy. "You sure there's a man here in Denver name of Nathan Kurlow?'' I asked.

Shad looked at me curiously and nodded his head. "Nathan Kurlow owns three saloons and a number of other enterprises here in town. He's been traveling lately and was said to have been involved in some kind of accident. I've heard his face was badly scarred.''

"It weren't no accident,'' I replied. "I surely meant to do that and worse if I could've.''

I told the deputy about the fight at the cabin and particular the fight 'tween me and Nate Kurlow. "He declared it war 'tween us, so I reckon I ought to just go take it to him,'' I said as I finished the story.

"What you've said doesn't surprise me, even though he puts on the front here of being an honest businessman. I've watched and I've heard things. Nathan Kurlow is a thief and worse.'' Deputy Shad rubbed his chin and looked at me close. "I'd ask you not to start anything with him here in town, Mr. O'Malley. It's my job to try and keep the peace, and I take the job seriously. Besides, Nathan Kurlow and the county sheriff, my boss, are the best of friends. No matter what happened you'd be in the wrong.''

''I'm not a mister,'' I told the deputy. ''My name is Matt to my friends, and since you asked me nice, I won't take it to him. But if he comes huntin' me, I'm surely gonna try and finish what I started at the ranch.''

''Understandable, Matt, and I'll help where I can.'' He dropped his hand to his gun in an unconscious gesture and then looked me in the face. ''Between you and me, I don't think my boss is all that happy he hired me. I'm an honest man and pride myself on being the best lawman I can be. I can't say the same of the sheriff.'' His hand moved away from the well-worn grips of his pistol, and he adjusted his hat. ''I have to get back to the office. The sheriff spends most of his time in Kurlow's uptown saloon, and I have prisoners to feed.'' He turned to leave, and I stopped him.

''I near forgot. My partner took this off the man that was shot last night. It ain't mine, and even though we could surely use it, I don't feel right keepin' it.'' I handed over the new gold money, and he looked at it curiously.

''We don't see much newly minted money out here. Might be something I can trace back.'' He stuck the money in his pocket and turned to leave. He stopped and turned back toward me. ''My friends call me, Shad, but only my friends.''

I nodded and figured he meant that I was counted among his friends. I surely hoped so 'cause Shad looked like he could bring down the wrath upon a man if he was stirred.

I watched him walk off, then turned and looked into the livery. Chris was rubbing down his brown and white paint, and a body could tell the horse just purely loved the attention. I often judged a man by the way he treated his stock 'cause I always reckoned that animals have feelin's just like people. If a man would mistreat a critter, then he'd probably mistreat people, and was no one I wanted to be around.

''Let's go get some breakfast, and I'll talk with Lee,'' I suggested to him.

Chris nodded and closed the door on the stall. He slapped his hat on his head, and we walked down the street toward The Rainbow City. My breath was comin' in short little puffs, and it felt like I had a stomach full of flies. First, I had to tell Lee what was really goin' on with Ara the night before, then I had to ask her the main question. I reckoned she'd probably go back to the Storm King with me, but you just can't be sure about a thing like that.

We walked in and the bell rang over the door soundin' our arrival. The sun was shinin' bright through the calico curtains makin' the place hopeful and happy. Uncle John and Tommy O'Neal had got in just before we did, and John looked a mite uncomfortable. Gettin' shot had a way of doin' that to a body.

I looked around for Lee, but didn't see her. We sat down at a table next to Uncle John, and I kept lookin' 'round. I reckoned maybe she hadn't come down yet, even though that didn't seem like Lee.

One of the servin' girls come out of the kitchen and smiled at us.

"You're lucky to be some of the first ones in this morning," she said. "We got fresh-baked biscuits, beef gravy, steak, eggs, and fresh apple pie instead of the dried apples we had yesterday. The apples just came in from the East with a trader."

"I'll take some of all you said, and a couple of gallons of coffee," I said, smilin' back at her.

The others ordered exactly the same thing, and she went walkin' back toward the kitchen. The new cook stuck his head out the swingin' door a few seconds after she'd walked through it.

"You better start with the pie," the cook yelled. "It's still hot, and once folks find out we got it, there'll be a run on."

He ducked back in through the door without waitin' for an answer, and the girl come back out with a steamin' golden-baked pie that give off such a smell that I near bit my tongue off.

"You seen Lee this mornin'?" I asked her as she set the pie down.

"No, and it's not like her. She's always up and has the coffee cooking before the rest of us get here."

I was gettin' fair worried about her and was serious thinkin' about goin' up the stairs to her room, which was over the dinin' room.

"She's gone, Matt," Uncle John said quiet-like from the table behind us. "She left last night."

I turned and looked at him and saw the truth in his eyes. I felt like I'd been kicked in the gut by a bull buffalo.

Chapter Six

"Lee came to my room just after you and Chris left last night. In fact, I had the feeling that she had been waiting for you to leave," John said quietly, without lookin' at me.

"She told me what she'd seen between you and Ara, and she was obviously upset. She told me she knew that you had once been close to Ara, but Ara would never marry you because of problems in the past." Uncle John took a deep breath like the whole thing was causin' him pain, and then continued. "Lee told me she felt like there must be something missing between the two of you."

"There's nothin' missin' between her and me," I said in a voice that sounded like it come from a whipped pup. "I told Ara that I was gonna marry Lee, and Ara kissed me good-bye. It was an innocent thing, but it just happened that Lee seen it. From where she was standin' it probably didn't look too good."

"No. In fact, she feels she's not enough of a lady for you. She's heading somewhere to get some polish. She said she is going to walk, talk, and act like a lady, just like Ara." Uncle John looked at me with serious eyes and put his hand on the table. "I would certainly hope that no nephew of mine would be playing lightly with the affections of a fine girl like Lee."

My back straightened, and I was sudden mad all over. I didn't say nothin' for a minute, lettin' the fury drain out of me. I reckoned only Uncle John, Pa, or my brothers could talk to me that way without looking down the barrel of my Colt.

"I love her, Uncle John, and I was gonna ask her to marry me today. I don't want her changin'. She's perfect just the way she is."

"She didn't say where she was going, Matthew, but you'd best go after her," he said quietly.

I stood up and looked at Chris. "No sense you trailin' on this one," I said to him, a little embarrassed.

"You know I will, *señor*, if you want me."

"I know, but this is a thing I got to do alone, and they really need you back at the ranch." I looked out the window, thinkin' out loud. "She can't have gotten too far. Trouble is, she might be headin' anywhere."

"She'd need some kind of transportation," John observed, "and she's smart enough to know better than to try and go alone. That means a stagecoach, since the railroad isn't here yet."

"I'll start with the stage station. I know there's one that goes out early mornin' everyday."

"You find out if she was on it, but before you leave, I want you to come back and see me," John said.

I nodded my head again and scooted back from the table. I turned, walked to the door, and pushed out onto the street with my head down. I hadn't walked twenty steps when a loud, coarse voice stopped me in my tracks.

"Look what we got here, boys. We got us an O'Malley, and he's alone."

I looked out from under my hat brim and saw Black Jack Fallon standin' right in my way. I felt a big smile come up on my face. What Black Jack didn't know was he'd tackled one heartsick feller, and he was just what I needed. I took another step and swung my right fist as hard as I could right into his ugly face. The blow sounded like an ax hittin' a hard stump, and he went over on his back.

"Stand back, the rest of you," a voice said from the boardwalk. "This is going be a fair fight. Jack asked for it, now he's going to get it." I looked over at Deputy Shadrach Taylor and grinned.

Fallon stood, wiped the blood from his mouth, and come at me with a rush. I waited 'til the last second and then fetched him a good thump right in the ear with my right fist. I followed in quick with a left to the gut, and then, as he bent over suckin' wind, I brought a right uppercut from down around my knees. I hit him square on the chin, and he was out cold 'fore he hit the street.

"Ah, lad, that was a thing of beauty," Holstein vest, Tommy O'Neal, said from the boardwalk where he stood beside Shad. I looked around and saw everyone had come out of the eatin' house to watch. Shad had his gun out and pointin' at Black Jack's three buddies.

"Pick him up and haul his carcass over to the jail," Shad told them.

"We didn't do nothin' . . ." one of them started to protest.

"Disorderly conduct, cussing in public, display of a firearm, assault . . . I could go on for a long time, fellas," Shad said. "You have been walkin' hard-heeled ever since you got in from back East. You just learned that we take our fighting serious out here, and we don't talk about it before we start."

"Can I go, Deputy?" I asked.

"You're free to go, Mr. O'Malley, and thank you for the entertainment."

I stepped around the small crowd and headed for the stage station at the end of the street. My hands hurt a little, but I felt some better on the inside.

The stage station was a new false-fronted building with a big corral behind it. The station man was small, bespectacled, and all business.

"She left out of here about two this morning. Most everybody knows Lee, at least in this part of town, and I was a little curious about why she'd leave on that particular stage. She didn't say why, but she did say that the Pinkertons had contacted her a few weeks ago and told her she had some relation somewhere back East. She told me she'd decided to go back for a visit. Sounded reasonable to me."

"She didn't tell you where she was goin'?" I asked.

"Nope, just that it was east. This stage went north, though."

"North?"

"Yep. Goes up to Cheyenne. From there most folks get on the train and head one place or another."

I thanked the man and started walkin' quick for the livery. I stopped and looked up the street toward The Rainbow City. I'd promised Uncle John I'd check with him before I left out. I chaffed at the delay, but a promise made is a promise kept.

I found them still at The Rainbow City drinkin' coffee.

"Looks like she headed for the train at Cheyenne," I said, pulling out a chair.

Uncle John pushed his cup back and looked at me serious-like. "If you don't catch up to her before she gets to the tracks, then chances are you'll have a very difficult time following her. It might be best if you come back here, and I'll try and find her with some of the resources I have at my disposal." He pulled one of them long skinny cigars from a pocket inside his coat and lit it up. He got it goin' good and looked at me again. "The choice is yours, of course, but you could spend a lot of time searching and never find her."

I looked curiously at him, figuring his advice was well meant, but really didn't hold much water. "I think you're readin' too much sign into it, John," I said. "I can catch up to her 'fore she even gets out of Cheyenne."

"Do you have any money?" he asked.

"Maybe fifteen dollars," I replied.

Uncle John stood up and unbuttoned his shirt. He stripped a leather belt from around his waist.

"There's three hundred dollars in there. One of the rules I always follow is to have more money with you than you think you'll ever need. A man never knows when an opportunity may present itself to turn a profit." He handed me the money belt. "Keep it around your waist like I do. Most bandits are in a hurry, and they'll miss a money belt if you get robbed. They settle for what's in your pockets."

"I don't know if I can pay you back—" I started to say.

"We'll worry about that when you get home," he said, cuttin' me off.

I stood up and put the belt under my shirt. It was heavy, so I knew it was big coin, not paper.

"Luck to you, boy, and keep your gun out of sight if you head east," Uncle John said.

I shook hands with all of them and headed out the door. I saddled Sin, bought a small bag of oats, paid my bill at the livery, and headed north on the main road to Cheyenne.

I made the dust rise behind me as I set a good pace north. I got to the first way station just after noon, and they told me I was on the right track. The horse-handler even described Lee. I watered my horse and took out after 'em again.

The way I had it figured I'd come to the next station sometime in the evenin', and Lee would be there gettin' supper. Most stages stayed the night at their main depots and had 'em set up to feed and sleep the passengers as part of the ticket price.

The sun was purty low when I pulled up in front of a flat-roofed, false-fronted building that had a sign out front tellin' everyone that this was Greely's Station and Hotel. I tied Sin off on the porch pole and stepped up onto the porch that went clear across the front of the big building.

"Howdy, can I help you with somethin'?" a dark-faced man asked. He was sittin' on a chair at the south end of the porch, and a Greener double ten-gauge with the barrels cut off lay across his lap.

"I'm tryin' to catch up with the stage that left Denver early this mornin'," I explained.

"Pulled outta here 'bout an hour ago."

"Pulled out?" I said. "I figured they'd stay here the night and leave again in the mornin'."

"Nope. That there stage is called the Cheyenne Express, and the only time she stops is to change horses and give the passengers a quick feed. They'll be to Cheyenne by noon tomorrow."

I leaned against one of the porch poles and looked at Sin. His ears was up, and he was ready to go, but I knew I couldn't do it to him. We'd already done something over forty miles, and I could feel him wearin' down. Much more, and I might hurt him so's he'd never be right again. I loved Lee more than anything, but I loved my Sin horse too. I cussed myself for leavin' my gray horse back in Denver. I'd counted on catchin' the stage my first day out, so I hadn't really come prepared.

"You got a horse I can rent or buy?" I asked the man without turnin' toward him.

"The only horses I got are the stage change horses. Can't neither rent nor sell any of 'em." I heard the man move in his chair, and I turned to look at him. He had the Greener pointed at me and was lookin' kinda strange.

"What be your name, mister?" he asked.

Now, most of the time it just ain't a polite thing to go askin' a Western man what his name was. I seen more than one fight start that way. There was a passel of folks in the West that were goin' by a different name than what they was born with. I wanted to tell him it weren't none of his business, but a Greener will surely make a man feel polite.

"Name's O'Malley. Matt O'Malley."

He visibly relaxed, and the Greener kinda pointed down at the floor. "I heard of ya, boy. You ain't no outlaw."

"No, I don't reckon to be. Fact, most of the O'Malleys always been people what liked the law, 'cept for a pirate or two back down the line."

"Man come in here ridin' in a fancy black carriage just after the stage left. He was a big man and figured himself for somethin' purty important."

"Name of Daniel Briggs?" I asked.

"That's the one," the dark man confirmed. "He met with a group of five men over there by the barn," he explained. "He left out back toward Denver in his fancy ride, and the other men come over to me. Said there'd be a man ridin' a black horse comin' along, and he was wanted for robbery and murder back in Denver. They give your description but didn't tag no name on ya."

"Why'd they say a thing like that?" I asked.

"I been known to shoot an outlaw or two in my time. Shot a couple here, and I was a sheriff back in the flatlands for a few years. I 'spose they figured maybe I'd shoot you and then ask you questions."

"You know who they was?" I asked.

"Don't know them by name, but they work for Nate Kurlow." He paused for a minute, looking out toward a barn that set across the road, then looked back at me. "I didn't trust their look enough to believe what they was sayin', and I trust Kurlow none at all, but a man out here alone can't be too careful."

I nodded my head in agreement. "Kurlow seems to be turnin' up everywhere I go," I said, mostly to myself. It was certain curious that Daniel Briggs and Nate Kurlow would see fit to meet out in the middle of nowhere. It was also mighty curious that they seemed to know what I was about, and that Daniel Briggs took an interest in me. Made me feel right important.

"Most folks think Kurlow cuts a wide swath, and they all want to hitch up to his wagon. I was a lawman too long not to be able to smell a polecat when he gets close. Kurlow has the look of bein' an outlaw with just enough brains and polish to impress certain folks."

"I keep hearin' his name, but I only seen him once. I know nothin' of his business affairs," I replied.

"Well, I hear plenty. I sit here on my porch and talk to people all the time, and they always got somethin' they want to talk about. Everybody thinks the West is a big place with no way of people bein' able to communicate very well." He laid the Greener on the porch and stood up. He looked back down the main road toward Denver. "The West is a big place," he said, "but folks is movin' from one place to another all the time. Lots of 'em come through here. Talkin' is the way most of the news is spread, and I draw a little money once in a while if I hear the right thing."

"How can you make money doin' that?" I asked.

"Some of your kin, if I'm guessin' right, pays me to keep my mouth shut about his affairs, and let him know if I hear anything interestin' about other folks' business. He told me once that information is what runs the world. I don't know how many people he's got out there like me, listenin' for the right piece of information, but he's a savvy man."

"Uncle John O'Malley," I said.

"I figured him for kin," the man said and smiled.

The sun was goin' down, and the crickets was startin' to sing. Both me and Sin was tired and hungry, and I knew I wasn't gonna catch up to Lee before she got to the train. I sighed, looked north, and then looked back at the station man.

"You got hay for my horse and a place I can keep him out of sight?"

"I do, and I reckon you might ought to sleep out in the little shed next to the barn. You got enemies, son."

I nodded and sighed again. I was feelin' 'bout as low as a body could get. I paid the man for the hay, and he told me the bed in the shed was free.

I was up and on the back of my horse an hour before dawn. There was a bite to the air that let me know that snow time wasn't far off.

I rode into Cheyenne the afternoon of the third day after I'd taken off from Denver. Sin was some wore down, and I was feelin' mean and ornery. I had no idea where Lee was headin', but I was still determined I was gonna find her and make things right. I asked questions of several people without findin' much out, but the main fella what sold the train tickets wasn't workin'. It looked as if I was gonna lose another day.

I slept in the loft at the livery with Sin munchin' some mighty expensive oats right below me.

The next day I got to the train station early, and the main ticket master was behind the little window sellin' tickets to all manner of folks. He was a medium-sized feller with glasses perched on the end of his nose. I reckoned bein' a ticket seller must be hard on the eyes since most of the ones I'd seen was four-eyed. He had a kinda superior attitude that always set my teeth up on edge and a whiny voice to go with his odious manner. I'd heard Owen say "odious" once, and I'd been lookin' for a chance to use it since. It surely fit this man.

"Yep, I seen her," he said to me when I asked. "Hard to miss a lady like that with all that red hair."

"You sell her a ticket to somewhere?" I asked impatiently.

"Yep, but she made me promise that I shouldn't tell nobody

where she'd gone, and most particularly not a young fella riding a black horse and wearin' a Colt's in a cut-down holster.''

Now, I'd been on the road for a spell of time. I'd slept in liveries, drank stale water from a horse trough, wore blisters on my back end, and paid about double for most everything I'd had to buy. I wasn't in no mood for some puny town boy givin' me a hard time. I held on to my temper, but it was a hard thing to do.

"Mister, I just need to know where she went," I repeated. "I ain't out to hurt her or nothin' like that." I was proud of myself for not slippin' my gears and tearin' his head off.

"I might be persuaded to tell you where she went if you wanted to know bad enough," he said in his squeaky little voice. He was rubbing his forefinger and thumb together in the universal language of bribes.

That just plain cut it for me. I grabbed him by his scrawny little neck and jerked him right out through the ticket window.

"Mister, I'm tired, and I been put upon by all manner of people during the last three or four days. I ain't in no mood to dig into my pocket and fork you out any hard-earned money just 'cause you got somethin' you think I want," I shook him a little to get his attention, and from the look of his big, round eyes, I'd say he was listenin' real close.

"I want to know where that lady bought a ticket for."

"Kansas City, but she said she was going on east from there," he managed to gasp.

I set him on his feet and brushed his waistcoat off at the shoulders. I leaned right close in his face and read to him from the O'Malley book of proper manners. "Next time someone asks you a polite question, you'd best answer," I said. "The next fella might not be a gentleman like me."

He swallered big and nodded his head. I let him go back into his little cage, and then I bought a ticket to Kansas City. I also bought passage for my horse on a stable car.

I was startin' to get some worried. I'd never been to a city of any size, and what Uncle John told me sat heavy on my mind. I might look all over and never come up with Lee. I didn't feel right about somethin' else either. I knew there was a powerful lot of work to do at the ranch, and no money to hire anybody to help besides them that we had. We had to get a lot more hay put up than we'd had last year, not to mention firewood, and other chores to get ready for winter. All of it was man-killin' work, and I knew I was needed back there. For right now, though, I had a destination, and I might be able to find out in Kansas City where she'd bought a ticket for. It was the only hope I had, and it was slim. I was startin' to get mighty discouraged.

A train whistle blew, and a conductor come into the station. "Twenty minutes for number nineteen eastbound," he hollered.

I loaded Sin on the stable car and went forward to a passenger car. I happened to glance back, and I seen a man dodge between the train cars. His actions seemed a mite strange, but then I didn't know a lot about trains. Maybe he was checkin' the brakes or somethin'. I swung up on the stair of the car and walked into the narrow aisle that ran between the seats of the car. There was already probably ten or so folks sittin' on the benches, and they was a mixed-up–lookin' bunch. I sat on a bench clear at the front where I could see the rest of the folks in the car. Most of 'em was tryin' to get comfortable and was payin' no mind to things goin' on around them. I always liked watchin' people, and sometimes made it a game to see if I could tell what they was doin' or where they was goin' by the way they acted and dressed.

"Boooard," the conductor hollered from the car behind us. I saw a couple of men runnin' to get on the last car, which was two behind the one I was in. I could see 'em plain and was purty sure I didn't know 'em, but I felt like I'd seen 'em before. Maybe it was just the type. One of 'em had long, greasy, yeller hair, and they was both carryin' rifles. They'd come from the stable car, so I figured they must have loaded horses. Just 'fore they jumped on their car, I seen the gent that had dodged between the cars join up with 'em. It was like he'd been tryin' to stay out of sight, so he wouldn't be seen. Fact, that was the way all three of 'em acted.

The train lurched as the engineer poured power to the drivers, and I looked from the window out across the town that had gained population and reputation while bein' an end-of-the-track town. It was a wild place, and all the men wore guns in their belts or holsters, and many carried rifles besides. It was the kinda town I was used to. I didn't reckon Kansas City and I would fit, and I felt a knot gather in my stomach as I thought on it.

I looked at the folks in my car again and cataloged most of them. There was a mother with two smaller children that was probably goin' east to see some of her family. There was a gambler that was playin' poker with a drummer that sat across from him, and behind them was a pair of cowhands that probably worked for the same ranch. Clear to the opposite end from me was a man sittin' by hisself that I couldn't place. His clothes was cow country, but his boots was expensive and hand tooled. He had him a fairly new Winchester, and he was carryin' two pistols instead of just one like most of the rest of us did. He had one in a special-made holster that hung from his belt and another in his belt on the opposite side. I just couldn't place what he might be doin' for a livin'. He also had a strangely familiar look about him. It was like I ought to know him, but I just couldn't place it. He tipped his head back on his seat, pulled his hat over his eyes. I lost interest and settled in to take me a nap.

When I woke, it was an hour from bein' dark, and I had a nasty crick in my neck. I could smell myself a little, which was somethin' I'd always hated, and my legs was cramped up from bein' between the seats. I was in no good mood, and I decided right there and then that trains was meant for folks with a lot more tolerance than me. I looked down the aisle toward the man at the other end and caught him lookin' at me. He looked away, and I couldn't tell if he was just curious or if he knew me. I remembered some of the recent happenin's and reckoned he might bear some watchin'.

Suddenly, the outside car door beside me flew open with a blast of cold air. Three men come in, and I could see plain they had guns in their hands. It was the same three men I'd seen actin' sneaky earlier, and I scooted over toward the window so I could get a better shot if it came to that. We'd just come up a fairly good grade, so they must've walked between the cars while the train had slowed. They wasn't payin' me no mind, except the guy on my end, who looked like he'd be lucky to be sixteen, was just kinda watchin' my direction. The other two was lookin' down the car to the fella with the expensive boots and two guns.

"Don't nobody move," the fella with the greasy, yeller hair yelled.

The young mother with the kids had been sleepin', and she gave out with a little scream when he yelled. Otherwise, it was plumb quiet except for the click of the tracks and wheels.

"How are you, boys?" Two Guns said in a quiet voice that barely carried to me.

"You know how we are, Taylor. You brought Harlan back from the nation, and Judge Reed hung him," the yeller haired one said loudly.

"That generally happens when you've murdered someone and robbed a bank besides," Taylor replied. "My job is to track down outlaws and bring them back for trial. I did my job, the judge did his."

"You had a hand in killin' my brother and being a marshal ain't gonna help you none," Yeller Hair shouted.

I was mighty curious about the whole thing. It was kinda interestin' to see somebody in a spot of trouble besides me. The gang with Yeller Hair was all pretty well armed, but they was greasy and dirty like they'd been on the trail for a spell. The man at the other end of the car was obviously a lawman of some kind, probably a U.S. Marshal. It was gettin' to be pretty plain that the two parties in the dispute didn't like each other. It also looked like the party of the first part, bein' Yeller Hair, was lookin' to kill the party of the second part, him bein' the Marshal. I didn't much like the odds at three to one, so I was seriously thinkin' about takin' a hand in the matter myself. Maybe I'd be a witness for the party of the second part, or some such thing. Or maybe I'd just shoot the outlaw closest to me and see what way the proceedin's went from there.

Chapter Seven

The outlaw closest to me was facin' my way, but was payin' me no mind. I thought maybe I could get the drop on him, but I couldn't see a way clear to take on the other two. I knew there could be no shootin' in the car. Things was close, and there was a good chance that one of the innocent folks would catch a bullet meant for a bandit.

"This train stops at Willow Springs to take on water. When it stops, we're takin' you off and hangin' you just like you done Harlan," Yeller Hair told the lawman.

The marshal didn't say nothin', but I could see he was lookin' for a way out. His eyes met mine, and I give him a sign to be watchin'. He give a slight nod and looked out the window. The train was slowin', and I figured we must be drawin' in to the place called Willow Springs.

The outlaws had taken the marshal's guns away, and as the train lurched to a stop, they roughly stood him up in the aisle. They weren't payin' no attention to me, so I stood up, opened the door to the outside, and slipped through. I jumped down and made a beeline for the cover of the willows that I figured give the place its name. I stood behind the thin line of trees that bordered a small spring and watched as two of the outlaws pushed the marshal down the stairs at his end of the car. The kid seemed to be hangin' back like he didn't enjoy what was goin' on. I looked toward the locomotive and saw they had the spout down on the water tank and was loadin' water in the boiler. I heard a burst of laughter and looked back toward Yeller Hair and his buddy. They'd knocked the marshal down, and Yeller Hair kicked him. The kid was still hangin' back. I got the impression that he weren't too pleased with what was happenin'.

I ghosted my way in their direction through the thin limbs and leaves. Willows weren't much for givin' a man cover, but the outlaws was so sure of themselves that I didn't reckon they'd think someone might help the marshal.

I come to the end of the willows and realized I was still too far away to do any good, so I ducked my head and started walkin' toward them. I made twenty yards before they spotted me.

"Where do you think you're goin'?" Yeller Hair hollered at me.

I looked up at them and grinned. "I couldn't help hearin' that you planned on hangin' a law-dog, and I figured to watch the fun."

I was walkin' as I talked, and I was gettin' up purty close to 'em.

"You stand your ground right there and let us get a good look at ya," Yeller Hair said.

I stopped, still grinnin', and then took two more steps 'til I was right up close to the kid. He was wearin' a filthy shirt and holdin' an express gun in his hands. He looked downright scared.

"We didn't invite no strangers to this party," Yeller Hair said. "This is a private matter, and I'd recommend you get back on the train."

I glanced at the marshal, who was bleedin' from the mouth. He was watchin' me close, probably wonderin' how I figured on pullin' this whole thing off. He'd have been some disappointed if he'd've known I had no idea.

The kid holdin' the shotgun wasn't payin' me much mind. He was watchin' the marshal and lookin' sick. I glanced at the other two and decided I might as well get things started off.

They was waitin' for an answer from me, but it appeared like the time for talkin' was over. I made like I was gonna scratch my nose and took the shotgun away from the kid. He weren't holdin' on tight and weren't expectin' nothin' of that sort. I reared back with the stock and brought it straight across, hittin' the kid behind the ear. The other two been purty certain they had the situation well in hand and wasn't worried 'bout nothin', specially some dirty cowhand with a stupid grin on his face. My move took 'em completely by surprise.

I dropped the muzzle of the shotgun down and fired both barrels with a single jerk of the triggers. Yeller Hair took the blast full in the chest, and it blew him back a good ten feet. The other badman was diggin' for his short gun at his belt, and I shot him twice with my Army. All of a sudden there weren't none of 'em left standin' on their feet.

The train whistle blew, and I turned around to look. The train was surely movin', and my horse was still on it. He was loaded on the car next to the caboose, and I thought I might just have a chance of catchin' up if I run. I started runnin' as hard as I could with my arms swinging, and my legs pumpin'. It was a distance of a hundred yards to the tracks, and I was fair winded by the time I pulled up even with the horse car. I jumped into the open door, rolled into the car, and threw my saddle out. I untied Sin and jumped onto his naked back. He laid his ears down and took a runnin' start. He jumped when he come even with the door, and when he hit the ground he near lost me and his footin' at the same time. He got his feet under him, and I turned him toward the marshal.

He was standin', watchin' me with a look of pure amazement on his face. All the outlaws was still layin' flat, and I figured I'd fixed at least two of 'em so they wouldn't do no more outlawin'. The one I thumped would probably be out for a spell since I'd hit him a fair lick.

I rode up to the marshal and slid off my horse's back.

"That was the darnedest thing I've ever seen," he said. He tipped his hat back on his head and tucked his thumbs in his gun belt. "I've never, in all my days, seen a cowhand run that fast, and I've never seen anyone jump a horse from a moving train."

He looked over my shoulder toward the tracks like he was seein' it all again and started laughin'. He laughed for a spell, got hold of hisself, looked at me, and started laughin' again. You'd never know to listen to him that I'd just fished his bacon out of the fire.

"I don't know what you're laughin' about," I said finally. "I saw four horses head over yonder hill when we started shootin'. I'd say three of 'em belonged to the outlaws, and the other was yours. I got me a horse, a saddle, and even a bait of food. With the train leavin', all you got is a bandit with a knot on his head and a long walk back."

The marshal quit laughin' sudden like and looked around him.

"You do have a point," he said. He looked at me again, and then his eyes dropped to my horse.

"Don't even think about it," I said to him. "I just saved your worthless hide, and here you are thinkin' about takin' my horse in the name of the law."

"It was just a passing thought," he said with a grin. He walked over to the kid outlaw that was stirrin', turned him over, and shook his head. "I bet he ain't turned sixteen yet." He looked back up at me. "What's your name anyhow? Seems I owe you a debt of gratitude."

"Name's O'Malley. Matt O'Malley from the Saguache Creek country."

His eyes opened a little wider, and he looked at me closer. "I heard of you," he said. He took a couple of steps toward me and pulled his hat down again to shade his face. "My name's Meshach Taylor. I'm a U.S. Deputy Marshal based out of Saint Louis."

It was my turn to get my eyes opened. I'd met Shadrach, and now Meshach. Seemed only fittin' that I make an effort to meet Abendigo.

"Where's Abendigo these days?" I asked.

Meshach looked startled, and then pointed off toward the east "Last I heard, 'Bendigo was working at being a marshal in a town called Ellsworth. How is it you know my brother?"

I told him the story about meeting with Shad in Denver, and he had another good laugh. He sobered up again and looked at the desolate country around us.

"It's a distance from here to anywhere else," he observed.

"It is that," I agreed. " 'Bout all we can do is hunker down and wait for another train to take on water."

"Might be a long wait," Meshach observed.

"It could be, but the other choices ain't so good."

He nodded in agreement and watched as the kid slowly sat up, holding his head and groaning. "Only good thing about this whole affair is that these polecats decided they wanted my rig. They threw my saddle, rifle, and bags out on the other side of the tracks. I got some irons in the bags that we can chain this fella with. You want to watch him while I go get my stuff?"

"Sure," I replied and moved to where I could watch the kid. He was probably two or three years younger than me, and I was wonderin' how he'd ever fallen into the company that he'd been keepin'. "What's your name?" I asked him.

"Billy Dean Sullivan," he said in a sullen tone.

"You one of the Sullivan clan from Missouri?" Meshach asked.

Billy Dean nodded and looked down at the ground. "You the one that shot my brother, Wade?" Billy asked in a quiet voice.

"It wasn't me, but I was there," Meshach said. "He wasn't much of a bank robber."

Billy nodded again, and the marshal walked off into the gathering dusk. He returned shortly carryin' a goodly load. He fished around in a leather bag tied to his saddle and pulled out a set of wrist irons that locked with a screw key. They didn't look all that comfortable, and I was some glad that it wasn't me he was puttin' 'em on.

I set about gatherin' the makin's of a fire as Meshach worked on Billy Dean. I had a beat-up coffeepot in my possibles bag along with some side meat and a loaf of three-day-old bread bought at The Rainbow City. I fried up the side meat in my old black skillet, then sliced and fried the bread in the grease left in the skillet. We topped it off with coffee strong enough to melt down a horseshoe nail. I reckoned I'd had worse suppers. I'd also had better.

"Don't I get nothin' to eat?" Billy Dean asked.

"You're dang lucky to be sitting up, let alone begging for food," Meshach said. "I still can't understand why O'Malley didn't shoot you instead of smacking you."

"He was standin' too close to me," I said, matter-of-factly.

Meshach nodded and looked back to Billy. "You see? You're lucky to be alive so the judge can hang you, instead of laying over there with your buddies."

"I ain't done nothin' worth hangin' me for," Billy said, obviously scared.

"Attempted murder of a federal officer will get you hung in any of the courts I've been in," the marshal assured him.

Billy Dean sat quiet, starin' into the fire, probably thinkin' about a rough hemp rope snappin' his neck. I'd near had the experience once, and it weren't all that pleasant.

"I didn't mean to turn out bad," he said all of a sudden. "Ma, she had great plans for me. She said I was always the smartest of the bunch."

"You should've listened to your ma," Meshach said. "I expect you're the only one of the boys left."

"Pa and Les was hung down to Fort Smith for stealin' horses, Wade got shot durin' that bank robbery when you marshals walked in, and Carl got killed by a bad horse six months ago. Ma said he'd a been hung one of these days anyhow. That leaves me."

"Too bad," Meshach said. "Your mom spent all that time and pain giving you life, and you go and throw it away."

Billy Dean nodded, and I seen his cheeks was wet. It was 'bout enough to make me wish I'd shot him instead of sittin' here listenin' to his story.

I looked at Billy Dean and then over to the marshal. "He always been bad?" I asked.

"I don't know," Meshach said. "There any good in you, Billy?"

"There was once. I was a good wrangler and fair with a rope. I worked down to Saint Joe for a while, then drifted up to Abilene with a herd from Texas when the pens opened there. I worked hard." He looked over at the bodies of his friends. "The one with the yeller hair was Dubby Colten. He thought himself a bad man, and started gettin' a gang together. Me, Dubby's little brother, Harlan, the one that got hung, and Goose Hawkins—he's the other dead one over there—was all there ever was.''

Billy quit talkin' and looked into the fire for a while. Then he started up again. ''We rustled a few head of cows for some drinkin' money; then, a week later, we broke into a mercantile for some whiskey. We just all kinda followered along with Dubby. Then they decided to rob a bank. Ma had writ me and said she was ailin', so I went home. They tried the bank while I was gone. They got forty-eight dollars, and Harlan shot the bank clerk, or so I heard. He had the bad luck to mount a slow horse, and you guys caught him.''

''Caught him just before he hit the breaks of the Arkansas,'' Meshach said. ''We'd never rooted him out of there if he'd made it.''

A small cold breeze hit us, making the fire sputter and sending sparks into the dark of the night. I shivered and looked across the fire at the marshal. He seemed lost in thought and Billy Dean was starin' into the fire.

''I have to think on you, Billy,'' Meshach said suddenly. ''I surely hate to hang the last survivin' son of a good woman, but I have a duty to do. I can't just let you go, and you have a lesson to learn that can't be learned unless there's some kind of punishment. A man is responsible for the decisions he makes, good or bad.''

Meshach fell quiet, and then stirred the fire with a stick. He seemed to come to a decision and stood up, throwing the stick onto the fire.

''First thing you're going to do is bury your buddies,'' he said. He pulled the screw key from his vest pocket. ''Lucky it's sand here,'' he commented. ''You can use Matt's skillet and contemplate your future.''

Billy stood up and held out his hands so Meshach could take the irons off.

It was a long night for Billy, and for me too. I was a light sleeper, and the noise of my skillet bein' shined in the sand made me restless. My mind was workin' too fast, and I was havin' some heavy thoughts about what I ought to be doin'. I was torn between goin' on east and headin' back for the ranch. I finally fell into an uneasy sleep.

I woke up 'bout two in the mornin', and the moon was glowin' gold right over my head. I looked around at the night sky and saw the Milky Way. I throwed my blanket off and walked out away from the light of the fire. Once I was well away, I looked back up at the night sky and the warrior's trail, what the Injuns called the Milky Way.

"God," I said quiet. "I ain't much on prayin', but I need some help, and if Kiowa and the Major are listenin', I'd appreciate them speakin' up too." I fell quiet and heard a coyote cryin' somewhere way out from me. It was a sorrowful sound and made the breath catch in my throat. "God, I'm stuck. You know I love Lee, and you know I got work to do back to the ranch. I got a feelin' if I don't go back, the partnership might have some real hard times. We might even lose all we been workin' for. I just don't know rightly which way to go. I reckon I'm askin' for some word from you or one of your friends that will point me in the right direction."

I stood there quite a spell, waitin' for a bush to catch on fire and start talkin' like what I knew used to happen in the old days. I'd been careful so's I wasn't standing too close to any of the tall sage case God decided to light one up. Ma'd always told me that if I prayed with true and pure intent I'd get me an answer.

Well, nothin' happened. I asked a couple more times and listened hard for a few hours more. It was startin' to get light in the east, and I reckoned I'd been out in the sage for quite a spell. I was fair disappointed, but I figured that God just wasn't up to talkin' to a sinner like me.

I started walkin' back to the camp, wonderin' what I ought to do, when I got a funny feelin' in my gut. All of a sudden, just as plain as day, I knew what I should do. I might love Lee, but my family needed me. There was a purty big question of if we'd even be able to get through the winter, leave alone lookin' any past that. We was broke. 'Bout all we had left was our strong arms, a few cows, and a will to work. I figured it might be enough to see us through, but I knew I was needed there. I was needed there now, not two or three months down the road when the snow was belly deep to a tall horse.

I stopped dead in my tracks. I come to realize that I'd gotten my answer. I studied on it a minute and figured that maybe God didn't talk to everyone from a burnin' bush. Fact, I was glad he didn't. I don't know quite what I'd a done if a bush started talkin' to me. I reckoned that maybe some folks, like me, got their answers quietlike. I looked up into the sky and watched as a bright, white cloud puffed itself up against the growin' light.

''Thanks,'' I said. I figured it was enough.

I got back to the fire, and Billy Dean looked drawn and pale. Bad enough he'd dug a sizable hole with a skillet, but they'd been his friends as well. I knew it hadn't been easy, but it'd been a lesson to him. He knew it could've been him down under that sand at Willow Springs. He'd remember that longer than he would just about anything else.

''You're up early,'' Meshach said as I walked in.

''Had some thinkin' to do,'' I said. ''I've decided to head back for the valley instead of goin' on east.'' I'd never told Meshach what I'd been doin' on the train and he hadn't asked.

He nodded and stirred some side meat in my now shiny skillet.

''Meshach, I got me an idea,'' I said to the marshal. ''Billy Dean don't seem like he's all that bad. Maybe we ought to spare his ma knowin' that all her boys ended up coyote bait.''

''What you got in mind, Matthew?''

''Parole him out to me. We got a big ranch over in the San Luis Valley. We're always short on help. I put him to work for wages, payable next spring, and from time to time we can check in with your brother Shadrach to let the law know how Billy Dean is doin'.''

I looked over to Billy and could see hope startin' to come up in his face. I thought I could tell that Meshach wasn't all that keen on seein' Billy hang, but I also knew he had a duty to the law. I looked to the marshal, and I could see a shine in his eyes.

''I don't know if that's entirely legal. . . .'' he said, and then hesitated. ''I guess I can live with that, but you got to promise me if he starts going bad, or he runs from the ranch, you'll hunt him down and shoot him. I can't be for chasing him all over the country again since I had him in my hands once.''

''You understand that, Billy Dean?'' I asked him.

He nodded and looked to the marshal. ''I promise neither one of you will ever be sorry you give me the chance. I make you that sacred promise right now.''

Meshach looked satisfied and stood up. ''He's yours now, Matt. If he don't turn out, I'm going to blame it on you.''

I nodded and looked to Billy Dean. I could see determination on his face, and I certainly hoped I'd made the right decision. I figured Meshach meant what he said about blamin' me if Billy Dean turned sour. There was just no way I wanted to have the Taylor boys mad at me for any reason.

''I plan on foggin' out of here,'' I said, ''but we're a little short on transportation. You got any ideas?''

''Doubt there'll be a train going west for a few days, but there's some friendly Arapahos that camped on the other side of the spring sometime during the night.''

I looked where he pointed and saw a small column of smoke comin' up on the other side of the willows.

''Wonder how come I didn't notice 'em,'' I asked, half to myself.

''Billy said you'd gone out into the sage right before they pulled in. He woke me, and I watched 'em set up camp. They knew we was here, and since we still have our hair, I naturally supposed they were friendly.'' He grinned at me, and I couldn't find fault with his logic. ''Point is they might be willing to trade or sell you a horse. It looks like they got a couple of extras. I'll sign a bill with you to prove that you bought it from Indians, so you don't get hung if somebody claims it once you get to Denver.''

The upshot of it was that I walked into their camp slow and made some friendly signs to the buck I figured was the top man. He motioned me to come on in.

''You need something? My name's Red Dog,'' he said to me in better English than I talked most of time.

"I thought you Injuns was big on smokin' pipes and such before you got to the point," I said with a smile.

"I'm not full Indian. My father was white, one of the early trappers that came out with the companies. They went back, but he stayed. He took my mother to wife and stayed with us for twenty years. Treated us good, and provided well for the family band. He was well loved by the entire tribe and much respected. Got killed trying to get some of our horses back from the Paiutes."

"Well, if we ain't gonna smoke a pipe, I need to trade for a horse if you got an extra."

"I got two. Which way you heading?"

"West."

"I'd say these horses would be good going that way. If you go east, say around Kansas territory, I'd take a different horse."

"You want to trade or sell?"

"We need money," he said with a smile. "We're heading for winter grounds and need to buy some staples for cold weather."

Time we got done dickerin' I bought both the horses for thirty dollars. I knew they was worth double that, but like I argued with Red Dog, they was only good for half of the country.

Red Dog laughed at my logic and let me have 'em. He had an old Army saddle that he threw in on the deal.

I walked back over to our camp leading the two horses and told Meshach about riding his new horse in Kansas. He laughed and gave me fifteen dollars. He tossed his saddle on the back of the bay mare he'd picked and turned back to me.

"It's been real interesting, Matt," he said. "I owe you a favor, and one of these days maybe I can pay you back."

"I kinda like havin' a lawman owe me," I said with a grin. "Never know when that can come in handy."

He climbed onto the back of his mare and headed off east.

"Let's get our stuff together," I told Billy. "We got a long ride ahead of us." Ten minutes later we was ridin' south by east.

We were gonna make good time. The grulla gelding I'd bought from Red Dog was a quality horse with good manners. He had a small diamond blaze on his forehead and three white feet. He was near as big as Sin and had an easy gait even if he was only good west of Bent's Fort.

As we was headin' out, I stopped Sin and glanced back at the twin ribbons of rail headin' east. I was missin' Lee somethin' terrible, and I knew that she'd left 'cause she was hurt. I still wanted to make that right, but I knew that chore would have to wait. I just hoped she didn't find some other man while she was East. That's the one thought that'd been on my mind from the time I started after her. Lots of things could happen, and there was a chance I'd never see her again. It made me sick to think that way.

I turned Sin's head back south. "We're headin' home, boy," I said to him quiet. He flicked his ears forward like he knew what I was talkin' about.

Chapter Eight

I had a feelin' I was bein' watched. It was more than a feelin' really. I was certain there was someone up in the timber watchin' the ranch. I'd caught a bright reflection from the slope early in the afternoon. Sometimes that'll happen from a piece of quartz if it catches the sunlight just right, but this wasn't quartz. I turned away and happened to glance over at the corral. All the horses' ears were up, and they were looking right where I'd been lookin'. If it'd been an animal movin' they wouldn't have taken much notice.

All things considered, I had more than just a feelin', but it weren't enough for me to get the whole crew in an uproar, not yet. In the meantime, I made sure I changed positions often and never stayed in an exposed spot more than a few minutes at a time. I wasn't one to forget new gold money and shots from the dark. It seemed reasonable that it was me they was huntin' if there was someone up on the side hill.

"That boy you brought back is a real worker," Dan said to me as I walked into the barn. He had his shirt off and was toppin' off a stack of new hay with a three-tined fork.

"I figure all he needed was a chance to be with some good company and folks that cared," I said, still looking from the open door to the side of the mountain.

"Well, he's a good one." Dan jumped off the stack, slipped his shirt on, and walked over to me. "We'd better get up to the cabin. It's nearly time for the meeting."

"You go ahead," I replied. "I'll be along directly."

At breakfast Owen had said he'd like to have everybody in the partnership take a break at three and meet in the shade of the

94

porch. He wanted to go over the accounts and decide what we was gonna do next. Dan started to walk off, then he stopped and turned toward me again.

"You heard of Daniel Briggs?"

"You mean the big frog in the Denver pond?" I asked.

"Seems he's come up to Saguache from Denver. Mears was up here a few days ago and says he just don't like the man."

"Well, Otto ain't the most lovable man in the world hisself," I replied.

Dan smiled. Otto had a small reputation of cuttin' corners. "I wouldn't think much about it, but John Lawrence also says that Briggs is walking hard-heeled around town. John has no use for him either."

Now that give me pause. John Lawrence was a man of uncommon principle and judgment, and one of the founders of Saguache as was Otto Mears.

"John says that Briggs is talking land sales and farmers," Dan continued. "Seems he's also talkin' that the O'Malleys have no right to all the land we hold."

"We bought and paid for all of our land here in the meadows," I said. "We got clear title with deeds and all. Ignacio and Ouray went with us to Denver and did the filin' legal."

"We know that, but I bet Briggs doesn't," Dan replied, lookin' off toward the main cabin.

"Hell, a man can't farm this country. It's too high and dry," I said.

"Maybe it's nothing," Dan said with a shrug. "It bothers me, though. Uncle John said that Briggs is hiring men. They look to be gun hands." Dan turned and walked on toward the cabin.

I watched Billy Dean swing a scythe against the tall stand of coarse meadow grass along the creek. We'd cut near all the hay that we'd irrigated out in the meadow, and we was havin' Billy finish up what we'd missed against the creek itself. We'd been home a week, and Billy had proved to me that he was a good hand. I weren't sorry I'd brought him home.

We'd been workin' steady from first light 'til well after dark every day tryin' to get ready for the winter. The ranch itself probably set about eight thousand feet, but there were mountains close about that were well over eleven thousand. We'd learned the hard way what the winters could bring, so we was tryin' to think ahead. We planned to keep the cows and calves in the big meadows that lay close about the buildings when the snow started flyin'. We'd put together several windbreaks, and Mike had built a sled usin' one of the old wagon boxes. We figured to be able to feed the herd from our stacked hay even if the snow got deep. Dan and Mike had managed to cull the weak critters and the bull calves from the herd. We'd sold them to the Army at Fort Lewis. We'd gotten some cash money from the sale, but it was soon gone.

Wedge, Christian, and Danny had built another cabin, and was workin' now on a third. We laid them out in such a way that when we built a fourth, they'd form a square with all the front doors facin' in. They was well apart, but still in easy rifle shot of each other just in case.

Things were takin' shape around the ranch, but somehow I didn't feel a part of it anymore. Dan had taken hold and gotten things done while I was gone. It looked to me that he'd kinda taken over the position of leader. It was only natural, considerin' he was the oldest. Owen was still kinda puny, but comin' along. Patty and Jessie May were cookin' for the whole bunch, plus jerkin' deer, elk, and occasional beef. They'd dried some sand plums, blackberries, wild strawberries, gooseberries, and anything else they could find to add to the variety of our stored grub. Mike and Wedge had been to Denver whilst I had been trekkin' in Wyoming. They'd bought a big freight wagon to go with the smaller wagon we had and filled both of 'em up with flour, potatoes, sugar, and other staples they figured we'd need to get us by. Trouble was, it'd taken near all our money, and we was as close to flat broke as we could get not countin' Uncle John's money. I'd turned it over to Owen when I got home.

Wedge and Jessie had gotten right close, and I figured there'd be a weddin' about Thanksgivin' time, and I was happy for 'em.

I guess I'd been feelin' sorry for myself with Lee goin' off. I was the youngest of the boys, and now that we was all back together, I kinda felt like the youngest. There was a lot of discussions goin' on that didn't seem to include me. I wanted to be happy, and I wanted all my friends and family to be happy too, but it just weren't workin' for me. I had a restless feelin' down in my gut, and I figured I was gonna saddle my black horse and head out for somewhere else come spring.

I looked toward the mountain uneasily, watchin' for sign of movement, then I looked toward the cabin. They was all gathered. The ones that had an interest in the partnership was sittin', talkin', and occasionally laughin'. Wedge, Owen, Dan, Patty, Mike, and me was the ones that had money involved. The others was workin' for wages, and the whole group knew we was havin' troubles. I didn't need to see the accounts. I knew there was too many of us and not near enough ranch to go around. There probably wouldn't be any payoffs for at least two years, and maybe longer than that. I just didn't think we could make it. Fact, I was sure we couldn't make it.

They could talk all day, but the dream was spent. We'd last out the winter, but come spring we'd have to sell stock to meet our obligations. Pretty soon we'd be sellin' off our profit. You can't do that for long and figure to stay ranchin'. I watched 'em all for a minute and decided I didn't want to go to the meetin'. We still needed meat, and I'd seen a couple of fat, spike bull elk up on the ridge that ran between the mountains.

I put a pack saddle on my mule, changed from boots to moccasins, and put on my buckskins. I snuck from the barn to the back of the cabin through the brush and went in the back door. I liked my Henry, but for real fine shootin' I favored Pa's front-stuffer. He'd carried it most of the years he was a mountain man, and I was good with it. I took it from the hooks over the door and got the possibles bag that went with it. There was powder, balls, caps, and patches in the bag, along with a nipple wrench and some soft flour sack material for wipin' the gun down.

I walked over to the table and wrote a big note that simply said "gone huntin'." I closed the door and snuck back to the barn. I loved the feel of the old rifle in my hands, and it made me think of Pa. I looked at the rifle in the sun and was still struck by the beauty of it. It was a half-stock plains rifle made in Saint Louis by Sam Hawken. The barrel had been browned and was showing silver on the ridges of the octagon from wear. It weighed a little over ten pounds, but was balanced so well a man hardly noticed the weight. It had a finely detailed silver dragon inlaid on the left side of the stock, and on the right side was Pa's name, Tirley O'Malley, done in gold wire, fancy script, and perfectly inlaid. Now that I knew about Pa's early silversmith experience, I figured he'd done the work hisself.

I loaded the Hawken with a hundred and thirty grains of powder, soaked up a patch good with spit, laid the .50 ball on the wet patch, and started it down with a short starter. I finished the job of seating the bullet with the ramrod, snapped a cap on the nipple, and laid the hammer down easy to half-cock. I grabbed the rope tied to the mule's halter and started trekkin' up the trail that eventually led to the top of the mountain.

It was a steep climb, and I took it slow, careful to watch around me all the time. I figured I wasn't only huntin' deer or elk, I was also huntin' sign that would tell me if there was somebody sneakin' 'round on our mountain. If there was, I surely wanted to see him first.

I climbed to a little outcrop of rock that stuck out of the side of the slope and stepped into the shade of a clump of aspens. There was a tiny cool breeze blowin' up from the valley dryin' the sweat on my face and rattlin' what few leaves was left. I stood a long time watchin' both uphill and down without seein' anything. I was 'bout ready to start up the trail again when I caught a movement from the corner of my eye.

He was a hundred yards away and slow movin' across the face of the slope instead of climbin' or goin' down. He was kinda small, had on a flat-crowned hat, and was carryin' a Winchester rifle. From where I stood the rifle surely looked new.

When he'd disappeared into the brush beside the trail, I tied the mule off to a quakie and snooped down to where I'd seen him fade. I didn't follow right on his tracks, but stayed slightly above him in the brush. I was good in the woods. I'd been huntin' near all my life, and I had a knack for gettin' right close to game.

I reckoned if I could sneak up on an elk, I could surely sneak on a man.

I crept maybe two hundred yards along the face of the slope 'fore I seen him again. He was standin' in the shadow of some pines and was lookin' down at the ranch. He surely didn't suspect I was up on the side hill, or he'd a been lookin' 'round instead of down. I did just like Pa taught me. I took one slow step at a time, makin' sure I wasn't steppin' on anything noisy as I slid through the brush. I also made certain I never looked at the man direct. Pa'd always told me that a man can feel someone lookin' on him if you held the stare too long.

I made half the distance to him and stepped in behind a big pine, catchin' my wind. I'd been near holdin' my air. I settled down and peeked out to where he was standin'. He was lookin' hard down toward the ranch, and now I could see down as well. He had a clear view of all the buildin's and meadows. He kinda shuffled his feet, changed hands with the rifle, and then sudden like, he was gone.

It caught me by surprise, him goin' out of sight that way, but I could still hear him. I started followin' along, keepin' track of him by the small noises. We'd gone about three or four hundred yards down the slope, when he quit walkin'. I stopped when he did. I couldn't see him, but he weren't far from me, and the brush had thinned out. I surely didn't want him catchin' sight of me, not yet anyhow.

I eased down maybe ten short steps and caught sight of him. He was in a patch of thin oakbrush, and he was steadily lookin' at the buildings below us. We'd come down the slope 'most as far as I'd walked up earlier, so we weren't far out from the ranch. I stepped around the other side of a mountain alder and looked down. There was at least a dozen horses in the yard, and I could see a man standin' to one side of the porch wearin' a Holstein vest.

Uncle John must have decided to come out. I'd wired him from Garland and told him I was headin' home. I didn't feel much like stoppin' in Denver to see him, so I'd cut through the mountains to the north. I'd told my brothers about him, and they'd been fair excited to think some of our kin was actually huntin' us.

I heard the man with the Winchester shuffle around, and I peeked at him again. He had the rifle to his shoulder, and he was takin' a fine aim down in the yard. I felt my nostrils flare, and I stepped out of the cover. I took a quick step that put me directly behind him and 'bout twenty yards above.

"I wouldn't," I said loud enough for him to hear me. I cranked back the hammer on the Hawken, and he heard both me and the hammer clear enough. He hunched his shoulders like he figured I was gonna shoot him where he stood. It was a thought, but then I ain't geared that way.

"Put the rifle down easy 'cause I surely hate to see a nice gun scratched up."

He laid the rifle down by squattin' and then standin' up again in one easy motion.

"Turn 'round slow, and your hands better be empty when you do. I wouldn't mind a lick putting a fifty hole through you."

He turned until he was facin' me. He was a weasel-faced little squirt with a nasty knife scar across his face. He was probably five years older than me, but I made two and a half of him. He was plumb ugly, looked meaner than a two-headed snake, and no question he was a back-shootin' sneak.

"What's your name?" I asked.

"They call me the Missouri Kid," he replied with a sneer.

I guess he expected me to recognize his name, but I'd never heard of him before.

"I don't know who you was fixin' to shoot down there, but that's all my friends and family, and I'm right partial to 'em. I think I'll just shoot you right where you stand 'stead of goin' to the trouble of walkin' you down the hill." I was tryin' to get a rise out of him 'cause he just didn't look worried enough to me. I had him dead to rights, and he still had that nasty grin on his face. It was like he knew he had an edge on me.

Maybe he wasn't alone. The thought hit me like a jolt, and I got a terrible itch between my shoulder blades. If there was somebody else up here in the bushes, I was in deep trouble. I was standin' in the open and made an easy target if there was some-body above us.

"You won't shoot me," he said. "You're just a kid. You ain't got the sand to do it."

I didn't dare take my eyes off'n him, but I knew he was up to somethin'. Suddenly, his eyes flickered, and he looked over my shoulder. I hadn't heard anything behind me, but I was surely tempted to drop on my belly and roll into the bush. I didn't, and Missouri was fair surprised.

He was well into his move when I shot him. The big ball took him square in the middle of the chest. He was flung backwards a fair piece, and when he fell, it was all loose like a broken toy. I walked over to where he was layin' and kicked the sleeve gun out of his hand. If I'd turned to look behind me, he've had me sure.

Missouri's breathin' was ragged and wet. I figured he wouldn't be breathin' real long, but it was a still a right mournful sound. His eyes opened, and he looked up at me.

"Name," he whispered. "Your name."

"Name's Matt O'Malley," I said.

His eyes opened wide, and he took in a hard breath. "Least I was taken down by a gunman," he said. It was the last thing he'd ever say.

I walked quiet back up to the mule and untied him from the aspen. I'd been thinkin' about the Kid while I'd been walkin'. I didn't want the name of a gunman. I'd fought with my guns, but many of us did. Our weapons were tools that we used like a rope or saddle. Nearly everyone west of the big river carried a belt gun, and many east did as well. I'd killed too many men, but I didn't see a one of 'em that I could've avoided. We lived and worked in a violent and sudden place, and without my guns I'd surely been a dead man several times over. The Missouri Kid had died on the side of a mountain without a friend to know it, and it seemed a stupid way to go under. I guess there was a lot of stupid ways to die.

I turned the mule's head around and was just about to go back down the trail to the ranch, when I realized somethin' was wrong.

I stopped still and looked close about me. Somethin' had changed since I'd left the mule tied. I squinted my eyes down, and looked about me again.

The pack was gone. I always put a small pack together 'fore I went huntin'. Usually it was just a little food, some water, and a bedroll in case I had to stay out overnight. The pack had been tied behind the pack saddle, and it was gone. I walked around to the other side of the mule and checked to see if he'd scraped it off on a tree. It wasn't there, and I really hadn't expected it to be. My knots had been good, and it'd been tied with nearly new rawhide.

The leaves where he'd been standin' had been stirred some, and there was still some dampness left. I careful-like swept some more leaves away and found the track.

I studied it close. It was a medium-sized moccasin track. I got that itchy feelin' between my shoulders again and squatted down. I couldn't see nothin' outta the usual, nor could I hear anythin' that shouldn't be there. The birds all sounded normal, and a gray squirrel bounced across the trail. Whoever'd got the pack was gone now. It might have been an Injun, but I didn't think so. Injuns don't often run alone.

The Utes had often told us about the sprits that roamed our mountain. Thunder Mountain was a sacred place for the Utes, and they left offerings to the gods at several places on the slope. I didn't set much store by haunts and such, and these were Ute gods. I didn't reckon they'd have much truck with the likes of me. I thought of the moccasin track in the mud and felt the hairs come up a little on my neck. Injuns was notional folks, and it might be that their mountain spirits was just like 'em.

I grabbed the mule's halter rope again and headed back down. I was gonna pick up the Kid, and I was gonna get shut of the mountain without lettin' too much slow me down. I weren't scared, but I could see no sense waitin' 'round when there was a job to do.

Chapter Nine

I created quite a stir when I led the mule into the yard, and Uncle John come right over to me.

"You okay, Matthew?" he asked.

"I'm fair," I replied, not feelin' much like talkin'. "He didn't get lead into me, though he tried. He was drawin' a bead on somebody down here when I took him."

Uncle John walked around the mule and looked at the dead man's face. "I'll be damned," he said in a quiet voice. "Jerry Wells."

He walked back around to me and waved for Tommy O'Neal to come over.

"Looks like Jerry was going to make his promise good," John said to Tommy.

"It appears to me that the lad took care of him for ye, Johnny," Tommy remarked.

"Jerry used to work for me," Uncle John explained. "I fired him when Tommy caught him stealing from the company. He told me he was going to kill me, but I didn't think he really had the guts to try it."

"Well, he was gonna do it from behind the bushes," I remarked.

"Even then, I didn't think he'd try. Matter of fact, I'd forgotten all about him. I fired him over a year ago and a few thousand miles from here."

Everyone gathered around, and John searched through Missouri's pockets. He come up with a locket that contained an older woman's picture and two hundred dollars in newly minted gold money.

103

"Looks like the price has gone up," I said.

John looked at me, nodded, and turned to Dan. "This is part of what I was telling you about, Danny. This man knew me back East. That's why I feel certain that the problems I've been having are connected to my business affairs back there. I surely need your help. I need family help."

"I don't know what we can do, Uncle John," Dan replied. "We don't have a penny left except the money you loaned to Matt."

"It's not money I need. I need people around me that I can trust. I have only one or two men that I trust with my life, and it's not enough. There have been at least three recent attempts to kill me. Since Jerry Wells got here to the ranch well ahead of me, it seems that someone knows my every move." He was quiet a moment, looking at the dead bushwhacker still hanging head down on the mule.

"You know we'll do what we can, John," Owen said. "We always stand by family."

"Nearly every dime I have is invested in my railroad venture, as well as the money of many of my friends. Someone knows how tenuous our hold is on the contract, and they also know that if I die, the contract is forfeited. It would then be renegotiated with one of my competitors."

"I 'spect you ought to stay here for a spell," Wedge volunteered.

"That's just it. I've reached a critical phase in the rail building contract. I can't afford to be out of touch," John said.

"We're getting close to being ready for winter," Dan said, walkin' around behind the mule. "You loan us your men for a week, and we'll be as ready as we can get. Then we'll go to Denver with you and watch your back."

"Some of these boys won't do ranch work. They figure themselves to be railroad men, and any other work is beneath them. The ones that won't work I'll pay off." Uncle John said. He was quiet for a spell, lookin' at the strong-faced O'Malley men standin' about him, and I could tell there was emotion on him. "It's good to have family around me again. I kind of shut my own boys out of my life after their mother left. I raised them, but they have no use for me.'' He paused a minute, lookin' at me. ''A man needs family.''

He looked at the dead man on the mule and shook his head. He turned back toward us. ''We pull this off, and I'll give the partnership a full one-half of my portion of the profit.'' He held up his hand as Dan and Owen started to speak. ''I know you didn't ask, nor is that the reason you're helping me, but that's the deal. I won't accept any arguments.'' He turned and motioned to Tommy. They picked a couple of John's men to bury the Kid, and then he walked the rest of them over to the barn. Ten minutes later several of them were headin' east, but there was six that stayed.

The next week flew by as we worked puttin' in the wood, hay, and layin' up more food. We were startin' to get a hard freeze every night now, and the grass cracked when a body stepped on it in the mornin's.

I went up on the mountain every day huntin', and I didn't see any more moccasin tracks. I still had the feelin' once in a while that I was bein' watched, but didn't see no sign of anyone. I collected two nice young bull elk and a couple of small buck deer. I didn't shoot does or cow elk, figurin' to leave 'em for seed.

A full week after Missouri made his mistake, I left for the mountain with Pa's rifle and the mule. It was a cold mornin', and our breath stood like fog in the still air. I started up the path like I always did, aimin' for the high-up hills where the grass was thick and the game still was a-hangin'. I was walkin' with my head down when I noticed a wisp of a trail I'd never seen before. The light was just right to show it up, and I could tell it'd been used during the night since the frost was some disturbed. I turned up the trace and started tryin' to make out tracks. If deer had been down the night before, I might be able to track one out.

I followed the little trail for a spell up the steep slope, and 'bout halfway up another trace joined up with it. It was plain to see that neither one of 'em had regular heavy use, but now that they'd joined, it was some easier to follow. It was still headin' for the top, but it had changed direction while it climbed. It was now headin' 'round the other side of the mountain from the ranch. I come to a little seep of water that popped out of the ground and trickled toward the valley. The water cut the path and made it wet for some distance on each side. I stepped across the trickle, looked down, and saw the track. I knelt down and looked careful.

It was the same moccasin track I'd found by the mule when my pack had been taken. The track was fresh, made surely this mornin' as I came up the trail. I reckoned whoever was up ahead of me had no idea that I was on the mountain so early, nor that I was on his trail. I'd never been to the backside of the Storm King, at least this high up. The Utes spoke of evil spirits that haunted the rocky, flat top of the mountain, and it was said that they drew their energy from the thunder. I put no stock in haunts, least not much. I reckoned whoever'd made the track was flesh and blood anyhow.

I walked the mule down the slope a few hundred feet, pointed him toward home, and whacked him on the butt. He took off at a slow walk, but I knew he'd get there. He liked the barn. I figured on huntin' out whoever was spookin' around on our mountain, and the mule would be in my way.

I started back up the path slow and careful. I didn't know if the man ahead of me was friend or foe, but I surely didn't have many friends. What ones I had were all below me on the ranch. I was breakin' a sweat in spite of the cold air, and I kept the Hawken balanced in my hands.

The trail snaked through a heavy stand of aspens, and there was now a sight of elk and deer tracks on it. The moccasin tracks were on top of the animal tracks, meanin' the man had been the last one on it. I stopped just at the edge of the quakies and looked up at the trail as it went across a naked shale slide. I was gettin' high up, probably above ten thousand feet, and the air was thin. The trail went across the slide and disappeared into a thick stand of green spruce, and I caught a glimpse of movement in the darkness under the heavy timber. I stood still watchin' the edge of the trees a couple of hundred yards away, but the movement didn't happen again.

I was caught between a rock and a hard spot. If I started across the slide, I was gonna be in plain view if there was somebody watchin'. If that person happened to be holdin' a rifle and was any kind of shot, I wouldn't get halfway 'fore he'd nail my hide. The slope was too steep to go down, and goin' around the slide and back up was out of the question. If I was gonna find out where the trail went and who the man was ahead of me, I'd have to get across the slide.

I hunkered down and watched close across to the other side. Patience was somethin' hard learned, and many a man had paid the price for movin' too soon. A slow twenty minutes went by, and nothin' moved in the darkness under the heavy timber on the other side of the slide. I was about ready to get up and give it a try when I sucked in my breath. There was movement again, this time comin' out of the trees. I moved the Hawken 'round to where it was comfortable to my hand and watched. Suddenly, a doe come walkin' out of the spruce woods. She was smellin' the trail and takin' a step at a time, lookin' around and twitchin' her ears. I breathed a sigh and let her move off. That doe comin' out of the trees showed me that there was no one waitin' for me. I made quick work of gettin' across the shale and worked my way up through the heavy timber. I broke out into a large, beautiful alpine meadow still covered with white frost. At the top of the meadow was a cliff face maybe forty feet high, and then the flat top of Storm King rose above the cliffs. I could see the trail plain, and the fresh moccasin tracks on the path were easy to spot. I watched ahead of me, but stepped up my pace. It was obvious whoever I was followin' didn't know I was behind him.

I got up close to the red cliff and followed the tracks around the curve that shaped the summit. I come to a blind corner and slowed down. I ghosted from tree to tree, watchin' to the front and stoppin' to listen regular. Suddenly, I smelled woodsmoke. I'd trailed the man to his camp, and right soon I was gonna know who he was and what he was up to.

I sneaked right up against the cliff face and started workin' my way around the blind corner. I stepped over a fallen tree and followed his tracks behind a giant rock that had fallen from above. The space between the cliff and the rock couldn't have been more than four feet wide, and as I come out of the slot, I spotted the house. It was obviously old, tucked in behind some giant trees where the cliff face made another turn, and appeared to have been made by wallin' up a cave with stone. There was a small drift of smoke comin' out of a natural chimney that vented at the top of the cliff, and the small door and window faced right at me. I decided to hunker down and watch. Patience was a virtue, or so Pa had always said. I'd waited maybe five minutes when the man come out of the cabin. I couldn't see him plain, but he was wearin' buckskins and had a full beard. He had a badger skin for a close-fittin' cap, and I could see the buckskins had some simple beadin' on them. I didn't see any horses nor signs that he had any. His beard was white in contrast to the brown of his face, and he carried the rifle in his hand like it was a natural part of him. He had a big bowie knife stuck in a wide belt around his middle, and when he turned, I saw a tomahawk stuck in the belt on the back. He looked like I'd pictured the old mountain men lookin'. No matter how he appeared, he surely looked like a hard man, and not one I wanted to tackle without an edge.

I heard a noise down the slope and behind the man in buckskins. He heard it as well and looked down the slope. He stood quietly a moment, then ghosted into the trees. The noise became voices and the sound of horses walkin' across slick rock.

If I moved, the man I'd been watchin' would surely see me, but if I stayed where I was, the riders would likely follow the trail and find me.

I started steppin' backward easy and slow. I was just about out of sight when I seen a horse break out of the trees. I stopped in good cover and watched the riders.

They surely looked ready and willin' to fight. They rode with their rifles in their hands, and a pair of riders was out front actin' as lookouts. There was only one set of folks anywhere near for 'em to fight with that I knew of. That was my folks back down in the valley. I didn't figure this pack to be friendly, so I took a step farther back, gettin' ready to head down the trail I'd come up.

They seen the cabin and pulled up for a look. I heard a shouted order, and the two lookouts rode for the little shelter. They pulled up in front and dismounted. One of the men kicked the door open and went inside. He was only in for a second and then come back out.

"Ain't nobody home," his voice carried to me.

"Take whatever there is of value and burn the rest," another man said.

A shot rang out, and the hat flew off the man who had kicked the door down. I stopped backin' and waited to see what was gonna happen.

"You gents go on about your business and leave my stuff alone. I ain't botherin' nobody, and don't plan on it, but if you keep on, I'm surely gonna empty some saddles."

The voice of the buckskin man had a flat hollow ring to it as it echoed from the cliff face. I'd heard the voice before, but I couldn't put a name and face to it.

I sighed and started workin' my way back up through the space between the fallen rock and the cliff toward the cabin. It looked to be shapin' up to a fight here on the mountain, and the odds wasn't much good for the old man.

I was some puzzled. The man livin' in the cabin surely knew we was in the valley, but he'd made no move to contact with us. It was a high, lonesome place he'd picked to live, and the winter would be pure hell. I admired his sap, which he showed by bracin' a small army by hisself, and I reckoned maybe I'd help him out if they decided to fight.

I moved back to the front of the notch, and the man that looked like the leader was edgin' his paint horse toward me. He looked small in the saddle, and he was carryin' what looked like a new Winchester.

"We're gonna kill you," the little man yelled toward the woods. "There's fifteen of us and one of you. You don't stand a chance."

Another shot came from the trees, and the man closest to the leader fell backwards off his horse. I could tell he was flat dead, probably head shot from the way he tipped over.

"There's fourteen of you now," Buckskin yelled, "and if you don't start movin' yourselves back down the mountain, you're gonna be next."

The buckskin man's voice was so familiar that I could almost catch who it was, and I had that feelin' in my gut that he was one of our friends.

The little man with the Winchester shifted his horse my way. "Get him, men," he yelled, and his gang spurred horses toward the woods and the old man. The little man on the paint horse suddenly slapped spurs, jerked his horse's head around, and jumped right at me.

I seen his face plain and dang near dropped the Hawken. It was Nate Kurlow.

His eyes flared when he spotted me. I don't know which one of us was more surprised, but there wasn't time to think, 'cause he was comin' fast. His hand raised the Winchester to fire, and I was two ticks behind him gettin' the Hawken up. It was gonna be close.

Chapter Ten

Kurlow was bearing down on me with his Winchester in his hand, held pistol style. I was still sheltered partly by the big rock and the cliff face, but a good shot could get to me. I held the Hawken loosely in my hands, waiting for the moment when he'd draw the horse in to take his shot. He hauled back on the reins, and the paint's eyes bugged out as he slid back on his haunches trying to stop. The frightened animal turned slightly and then reared just as Kurlow shot, causing him to miss. I touched off the Hawken shooting from the hip, and missed as the horse crow-hopped. Kurlow ripped his horse's head around to face me again and raised his rifle. My hand dipped for my Colt. I knew instinctively that he was gonna get his shot off first.

I could hear shots and shouts from the rest of the gang attacking the tree line as my pistol came level. I saw his rifle blossom with fire and felt a stunning blow on my left side. I touched off my shot and saw Kurlow wince. He fell backwards as the horse reared. He pulled his pistol as he climbed to his feet, and I run toward him. I wanted him, gun, knife, fist, I didn't care. He shot hit the rock next to me, causing me to flinch. I shot again just as he dodged to one side. He went out of sight around the corner of the fallen rock, and I rushed out expecting to be met with gunfire.

He was gone. The riders had massed and were retreating the way they'd come. Nate Kurlow was up behind one of his men on a big bay horse, and he was out of range of my Colt. I could see his left arm was bloody. I heard a shot from the woods, and another of Kurlow's men lurched from the saddle, fallin' heavy. The old man in buckskins was still fightin' and makin' his shots

111

count. Three of the riders spun around at Kurlow's command and headed for me. They had rifles and were makin' dust jump around me as they came on a dead run. It's a tricky thing shootin' from the back of a runnin' horse. More often than not a man can't hit a thing. I stopped and waited on 'em. They was still out of reach of the Colt.

"Kill him," I heard Kurlow screech over the sound of the shots and runnin' horses. They got close enough, and I tipped the Colt up. I slipped the hammer, and a man tumbled from the saddle, his horse runnin' free. I changed my aim and nailed another as they bore down on me. The remaining man took a slash at me with his rifle as he rushed by and hit my forearm a stunning blow. I dropped my pistol and made a grab for my knife. The killer spun his horse around behind me and pulled his feet up to kick the horse with his huge roweled spurs. Suddenly, he got a funny look on his face, and his feet dropped to the sides of his horse. He toppled from the saddle and landed on his face. A slim-handled knife stuck from his back, and Chris Silva stepped from behind the big rock. I reckoned now I knew who had been behind me on the trail them times I felt like I was bein' watched. He probably didn't want me feelin' like I was needin' a keeper so he'd stayed out of sight. I was surely grateful that he'd seen fit to tag along.

As Kurlow disappeared down the trail, I looked to see where I'd been hit. Instead of droppin' the Hawken after shootin' at Kurlow, I'd held on to it with my left hand. The rifle bullet from Kurlow's Winchester had struck the buttstock of the Hawken and probably saved my life. The bullet had drilled a neat hole into the hard wood of the stock, and the gun had smacked me a good lick in the side, makin' me think I'd been shot.

I loaded the Hawken, hearin' Pa's words in my ears about seein' to the loadin' of my rifle. I thought of the old man down in the trees and looked down the slope.

He was standin' a long step from the trees out in the open and was lookin' up at me. I waved my arm to show I was friendly and started working my way toward the cabin. Chris had caught up two of the dead outlaws' horses and was followin' close behind me, ridin' his own horse. There was five bodies layin' out in the small meadow. We'd trimmed 'em down some, but I figured they might be comin' back. If they hadn't seen Chris, they'd still think there was only two of us, and ten men ought to be able to take two.

Whoever the white-bearded man in buckskins was, he was right salty, and a good shot. I stopped in front of the cabin and waited. The old man had gone out of sight as he worked his way back up the slope from the trees. Abruptly he stepped from around the corner of the cliff face and looked me full in the face.

"Howdy, son. My name's Tirley O'Malley, and I most surely appreciate yer help." He seemed a bit unsteady on his feet and swayed as he took a step.

I swallered big, and looked Pa in the eyes. I saw no hint of recognition, but I could understand. I was a lot bigger and some years older since he'd walked down our farm lane headin' for the war.

"I'm Matthew O'Malley, and I reckon I'm your youngest boy," I said quiet-like.

I saw his eyes go wide as he looked me over, and then he looked at the Hawken. He'd carried the Hawken for years, and he knew the rifle the instant he saw it.

"I'm sorry for the hole in the stock, Pa. Kurlow near got me."

"Who'd you say, boy?" Pa asked, his voice showing emotion.

"Nate Kurlow was the weasel leadin' that pack of wolves. He's my sworn enemy."

"He's an enemy to all the O'Malleys, if I know the family."

"It's the same family," I said. "Danny told me the history between us and the Kurlows."

"You're with Dan?" Pa asked. He was havin' trouble catchin' up with everything I was tellin' him, and his eyes weren't focusin' good.

"We're all together in the valley, Pa. Down in the meadows where the cabins are."

"I can't believe it," he said. "I been that close to my family all this time, and I didn't even know it." He swayed again and pitched forward. I grabbed him and lowered him to the ground.

"He is hit, amigo," Chris said from behind me. He'd ridden up while Pa and I had been talkin' and was sittin' his horse. He was holdin' the other two horses he'd caught waitin' for me and Pa to get done.

"I reckon they got one into me, boy," Pa said in a weak voice. His eyes closed as I began to look him over for the wound. It was down low and mean, right at the top of his right hip. He'd bled a good bit, but inside his clothes where I hadn't noticed. I ran to the little cabin, found a tin bowl, and poured some water in it from a bucket inside the door.

I washed the wound quickly and then bound it best I could. He woke up 'bout the time I was gettin' done.

"We got to go, Matt," he gasped. "They'll be back, and they mean to kill us." Pa looked toward the cabin. "All I own is in that shelter, but there's nothin' there I cain't live without 'cept your Ma's locket. It's on a shelf toward the back wall. If you'd get it I'd be obliged."

"Can you sit a horse, Pa?" I asked.

"You get the locket and get me on the horse. I'll ride it to hell if need be." He took a deep breath as the pain hit again. "You'd best hurry, boy," he said in a quiet voice.

I helped Pa crawl into the saddle while Chris held one of the horses he'd snatched. Pa was gray around the edges, and it was plain to see that he weren't feelin' up to much.

I ran to the cabin and walked straight to the back wall. The room couldn't be over twelve feet by twelve feet, but big enough for a man alone. I found the locket and a small stack of papers on the shelf. I put the locket around my neck and shoved the papers in my shirt. I ran back to where Pa and Chris was waitin'. Pa was awake, but barely. I didn't like the way he was breathin', and his color was gray as a winter sky. Gettin' shot by a big-caliber rifle was a shock to the system, and at his age it could well be the death of him. We was high up on the mountain, and it was a long, rough way home.

"I hear them, my friend," Chris said. "If it were only you and I, we would stay and teach them that it is not wise to attack the O'Malleys . . . or the Silvas." He smiled when he said it, but

I knew he was serious. "As it is, *señor*, we cannot stay and fight."

I nodded in agreement and turned the outlaws' horse I was ridin' for the way back. After we got lined out, I put Pa on the trail in front of me where I could watch him. There was a time or two when I thought he was gonna fall, but he stuck in the saddle like he was glued to it.

I'd picked up the new Winchester Kurlow had dropped, I'd reloaded the Hawken, and I had my pistol. Pa was carryin' a rifle and a pistol, and Chris had a rifle and two Navy Colts, so I figured us good for a little lead in the air if it come to that. Watchin' Pa in the saddle made me figure it hadn't better come to a fight. He weren't up to it.

We crossed the shale slide. Pa pulled up, and I rode up even with him. "We can't stay ahead of them, Matthew." He was right, of course. "There's trail up at the cliff face near the summit. It works its way around to the other side. We may lose them if we take it."

What he said made sense, and we needed to gain some time. We turned up through the heavy aspens heading back for the summit. We was followin' a ghost of a trail I hadn't spotted when I'd come through the grove the first time. Chris was settin' a stiff pace goin' up the steep slope, and the horse I rode was the worst of the three. I started to lag behind, and I could feel the itchin' startin' between my shoulders again.

I knew what Pa was thinkin'. The men behind us would be slowed down by the slide, just as I had been when I'd come up. They'd be thinkin' that it was a great place for an ambush. They'd also figure we was headin' down the main trail toward the ranch as fast as we could. I expected Kurlow to surely have a portion of the men try and cut us off. By headin' up, toward the summit, we'd not only throw 'em off, but also get above 'em.

We broke out of the trees, and I could see the summit not far above. I heard a shot behind us, but the bullet hit nowheres near. It's a right tricky thing shootin' up a hill. I looked back and saw what I figured was about half of Kurlow's men back down the slope. He'd split his force, and they was surely huntin' us hard.

We come up against the cliff face that marked the beginning of the flat-topped summit and started to work our way around the upthrust of rock. Pa stopped a minute and looked at me.

"This trail loops around the base of the cliff face, and it'll take us to the other side of the summit. I used to know where there was a trail over there. It's a way to get to the meadows," Pa said. He was lookin' a mite better.

I nodded and followed close after him. Chris must've noticed us stopping, and he was waitin' on us. We caught up to him, and he led off again. We rode for a spell. Finally, Pa stopped a minute to get his bearin's. I moved up beside him.

"It's here close," he said, looking up the cliff. Since the top of the mountain was round like a mesa top, we was always goin' around a curve. "It's been maybe forty years since I rode it, but I know we're close." He was lookin' still better like maybe the chase was givin' him some new life. "The Utes say there's a way to get up on top, but I never been able to find it," Pa added. "Their stories say the trail is hidden, and the top of the mountain is full of haunts and such."

I was itchin' to get movin', but I knew there was no hurryin' Pa. I looked again behind us, and then turned a little to my right. I couldn't see but ten feet 'cause of the curve of the cliff. I caught movement from the corner of my eye. My pistol was comin' out as the two riders came 'round the cliff face behind us. They tried to bring their rifles to bear on us, but I was ahead of 'em. I shot four times, and ten seconds after I'd spotted 'em, both men was lyin' dead in the sand. I hadn't had time to even think. It was just a reflex action.

Pa kicked his horse, and we took out around the rock face in front of us.

Pa shouted and pointed, then turned down a trail that was barely visible. I kicked the plug I was ridin' in the ribs.

Chris was dodgin' and snakin' downhill through the trees at a dead run, and I was hard pressed to keep up with him. He'd always been a good rider. He rode down the slope like a crazy man. He was in complete control of the horse he rode, and Pa was close behind him, lurching in the saddle, but still ridin'. I was fallin' behind again, and I heard a shot not far from us. The horse I was ridin' stumbled and then fell. He was dead before I touched the ground. I'd kicked my feet loose from the stirrups and rolled as I hit, then jumped to my feet. I saw Pa and Chris disappear into the heavy timber, and then I heard a shout behind me. I looked over my shoulder. There were four or five men just breakin' over a small rise in the trail, and they had their rifles pointed my direction.

Now, shootin' while you're on a horse runnin' flat out is a chancy thing. I'd heard tell of a man who'd been chasin' a deer on horseback one time. He was takin' shots at it with a pistol as he rode at a full gallop, and his horse stepped in a shallow hole just as he took a shot, the pistol dipped down, and he shot his horse right 'tween the ears. I reckon the deer got away, though I never did hear for sure.

The boys behind me was shootin', but they was a ways back, and they was ridin' full out. They was just about as busy tryin' to keep their butts in their saddles as they was trying to shoot me, and none of the shots come close. I dove into the thick oakbrush where no rider was gonna follow and headed back up the hill on a dead run. The brush tore at my face and ripped my shirt near off me. They would surely expect me to go toward the ranch, so the top of the mountain was my best bet. I could only hope that Chris and Pa had a good enough start to get to the ranch before the killers caught up to 'em.

I made hard work of gettin' up the hill and stopped just as I came to the cliff face that formed the summit. I stood for a minute, catchin' my air, and looked close about me. There was nary a sound 'cept a robber jay hoppin' through the leaves under the aspens. I stepped into the clear and began working my way along the rock face. I was hopin' to find the trail to the top that Pa had told us about earlier, but I reckoned there was little chance.

I found it near by accident. I saw several deer tracks that was pointed at the cliff, and I followed 'em along a few steps. I found a narrow split in the rock hidden by a pinyon tree that had to be centuries old. The deer had walked straight into it. I stepped into the deep shadows in the cleft. It surely didn't look like a trail from the outside, but inside of five minutes I was on the top lookin' down at six heavily armed riders below me. I'd taken the time to hide my tracks as I headed into the split, and I didn't think it was likely the polecats below me was hunters enough to scout out my trail. I could probably have taken two, maybe three of them before they got to cover, but it would give away my position. I was glad the trace to the top of the mountain was a secret, and I meant to keep it that way. I stepped quiet away from the rim and walked toward the center on the flat-topped summit of Storm King Mountain. I walked around a small grove of trees and come face-to-face with an upthrust of red rock. It had little caves and holes carved in it by generations of wind and blowing sand. In each one of the caves and even in some of the small holes, the Ancient Ones, the Cliff Dwellers, had built masonry walls. It was a spooky feelin' lookin' at work that still existed after maybe a thousand years. It was no wonder the Utes stayed away from Storm King. They was mighty touchy about haunts and such like. I walked around the upthrust, lookin' into the walled-up caves. There was black-and-white painted clay pots, diggin' sticks, tiny corncobs, and animal bones scattered about. It was near like the folks had just left for a walk and might be back anytime. I even seen a pair of sandals made out of some kind of fiber. Kinda made me feel right peculiar. The wind was blowin' up from the north, and as it hit the short cedars, it sounded like voices whispering. I reckoned I'd seen enough around Hotel Rock, so I taken out toward the other side of the summit. I weren't spooked. I'd just seen all there was to see.

The flat top of Storm King was maybe a thousand acres of scattered cedars and pinyon pines. They weren't thick, but they did stop a body from seein' very far if you was down among 'em like I was. I come to a little clearing at roughly the center of the mountain top and stopped dead in my tracks. The rock was completely clear of any growin' thing, and right in the middle was a depression, more of a hole, that was maybe two feet deep by thirty or forty feet across. There was a wooden pole stuck into a hole that had been drilled in the bedrock and located in the heart of the depression. I'd heard tell of such things, but this was the first time I'd ever seen one. The device was proof that the old-time Spaniards had been on top of Storm King. They'd used the slick-rock to grind the gold out of the rock-ore. I walked around the depression and picked up several pieces of ore that still contained small pieces of gold.

I walked on toward the rim and come on another rock upthrust. This one, unlike the other one with the ruins, which I'd taken to callin' Hotel Rock, had just one cave in it. It only had room for one cave 'cause it was a big one. The front of the large cavity was maybe eight feet high and twelve feet wide. It weren't a cave like what I'd seen a time or two in the East. This was more of an overhang with a brow over the front. It looked to get higher on the inside than the opening was and was maybe forty feet deep. It was big enough to give good shelter to a fair-sized group of people. There was a short wall of laid rocks at the front of it, and it was higher than the ground in front of it, so I couldn't see in. I hiked up and took a peep inside. I sucked in my wind and near fell backwards at what I saw. I got hold of myself and looked closer. There was a half-dozen skeletons, and they still had most of the old armor and iron hats on 'em. There was swords layin' scattered about, and at least two of the skulls was off a ways from the skeletons still contained in the tin hats, telling me that someone had cut their heads off. There was arrows about, a few stone-headed battle-axes, and big dents in much of the armor. Whoever these old boys had made mad had surely gotten even with 'em. I stepped back out of the cave and walked back down the little slope to the flat of the mountaintop.

I settled down close to a wind-torn cedar tree. I let the sun beat down on me and thought about the Spaniards dyin' a long ways from anyone that knew or cared about their passin'. I was high up, and earlier in the day it had been downright cold. Now, with the sun high in the sky, it was warm, and I was getting sleepy. I was so hungry I figured my stomach thought my mouth had quit workin'. There was no help for it. I watched an eagle way high above me against the blue of the late fall sky and thought about what a mess my life was. Somewhere along there I fell asleep.

The cold woke me, and I realized that the sun was way down in the sky. I'd slept most of the afternoon away. I checked my guns over, surprised that I'd had the presence of mind to hang on to the Hawken when the horse had gone down even though I'd lost the new Winchester. I wiped my pistol off with my bandanna and laid it easy into my holster. I hoped I wouldn't have need of it, but I'd made up my mind to go home, and I wasn't about to let anythin' or anybody stop me. I knew for double-darned sure that I wasn't gonna stay on the top of Storm King over the night. It not only would be cold, but the wind was whisperin' again, and if I listened close, I could near hear words bein' spoken. I'd've rather faced a whole army than stay on top of the mountain in the dark.

I stepped to the edge of the cliff and listened for a spell. I could hear nothing 'cept the quiet sleepy sounds of birds settlin' in the trees and the quiet talkin' wind behind me. I went to the trail in the split rock and checked for tracks. Mine and the deer were all that showed in the sand. I took a slow step down, knowing that the cut in the rock was a perfect place to nail me, if they'd found it. I stood still a long moment at the spot where the cut opened up on the down-slope, then I sprinted into the aspens that grew close to the cliff. I stopped again and gathered my breath. I headed for the ranch, knowing full well it was gonna take me some hours to get there on foot.

An hour of quiet walkin' brought me to a spot that I recognized, and shortly I joined the main trail that I'd hunted on during the fall. The light was almost gone, but I wasn't as near as worried like I had been when I'd first started. I'd seen nor heard nothing of the outlaws, or anyone else for that matter, and I'd started to relax.

I hiked another good hour and stopped beside a little spring where I'd taken many a drink during the past year. I drank deep and long, then started down again

I nearly walked in amongst 'em. They was laid out around a tiny fire, drinkin' coffee and eatin' what looked like hard beans on blue tin plates. Two of 'em had blood showin' where they'd been nicked up. They was a nasty-lookin' crew, and neither Kurlow nor Beck was with 'em.

I made one slow step forward and then another. These men had chased me and mine all over the side of the Storm King. They'd shot at me, shot my Pa, killed a horse that wanted no more than to give his best, and were probably guilty of a multitude of other sins not known to me. I made another step that took me into the firelight, and I started seein' a reaction. A man across from me got a look of pure stark terror on his face as he realized what he was lookin' at. It was like he was seein' a ghost steppin' straight from the gates of hell. Another man clawed for his pistol in his waistband, and I killed him with the Hawken. The roar of the big rifle echoed down the mountain as the man was thrown over onto his back. I had the Army in my right fist, and I was figurin' on killin' them one and all. They must have seen it on me. They never twitched. Not a one of 'em dared breathe. I was cocked and primed, and they knew it.

"Gentlemen, I'm gonna read to you from the book of the O'Malleys," I said in my best preachin' voice. "You've sinned greatly this day, and you all just nearly paid the price as did our poor departed brother layin' there in the bushes."

Well, I settled in then and spoke to 'em about how it was sinful to come against the O'Malleys. I told 'em how the price of sin was death, and if'n I ever seen nary a one of 'em again, I was gonna start them on their way to heaven or hell. I told 'em it didn't matter if they was comin' at me or ridin' away. It didn't matter if I seen 'em in a store, in a saloon, in church, or just on the street. If I seen 'em at all, anywhere, anytime, I was just gonna figure they was there for me or mine, and I was gonna send them to bar of judgment and let the Lord sort out their sins.

I carried on for near a quarter of an hour, and time I was through, they was pure believers.

"Take your short guns out mighty careful and lay 'em down close to the fire," I said, most serious-like. They did, and they was careful. The jasper I'd scared at the first even threw his knife down without me askin'.

"Now, head down the hill, and when you get to the bottom,

you turn straight to the right. You walk long enough, you'll find somethin' or someplace.''

''Mister, I got me a horse I surely hate to loose,'' the scared fella said.

''You should've though o' that 'fore you come along with Kurlow. I just cain't find it in me to feel sorry for ya.''

They didn't say nothin' else. They took out without a look back over their shoulder. I gave 'em a good hour while I drank most of the coffee and ate what vittles was left. I gathered up their truck, then found and loaded their horses. The scared man was right. If the Morgan was his horse, and I figured it was since it was the best of the bunch by far, then he was surely gonna miss him. I knew of only one horse in the whole country that was any better, and he was down in the barn at the ranch. I tied the rest of the horses off in a string behind the Morgan and headed slow down the mountain. I wanted to know if Chris and Pa had made it, but the way things had been goin' of late, I was scared of what I'd find when I got home.

Chapter Eleven

I come into the ranch late, and my tail was near draggin' the ground I was so tired. The boys heard me comin', and they stepped out of the shadows when they seen it was me. They all had their rifles in their hands.

"Ah, *amigo mío*," Chris said as he walked up and took the spare horses from me, "I was just preparing to return to the mountain and find you."

"When did you make it in?" I asked him.

"Your father knows this mountain as well as any man could. We took a trail that went around and then down. It was much longer, but safer. We arrived only a short time ago."

"How is he?"

"It was a long trip and he is tired, but he is very much the hombre."

Pa and the other brothers had already done their huggin', and Owen had introduced Pa to the rest of the bunch 'fore I got in. From what I could see, they was all gettin' saddled up to come and get me. Made a body feel warm all over just to think they'd head up the mountain in the cold and dark to find me.

We led the horses into the barn and took the tack off 'em. There was a couple lanterns lit, and after the cold of the late night air, the barn felt warm. We got the horses taken care of, with some going out in the corral and some into stalls, and then we kinda stood around in a circle just lookin' at each other. Patty had looked Pa's wound over and bound him up when they'd gotten in, but he was still wobble kneed and sat down on a barrel. He looked purty spry considerin' the kind of day we'd had. The lantern light was uncertain and left some of the faces in dark and some softly lit.

"I didn't think you were still alive, Pa," Danny said straight out. He'd never been much for mincin' around with words. "Fact, we all thought you'd gone under during the war."

"You know I'm too damned ornery for a little old war to take me down," he smiled. "I got touched up a little, but nothing near as serious as what the Blackfeet done to me in '34."

"Where you been since the war ended?" Dan asked the question that had been sittin' frontmost on my mind.

Pa looked us all over and then looked back at Dan. "I 'spect I owe you all an explanation," he said. He stood, rocked on his heels a mite, and retrieved his rifle where it leaned against a stall door. He turned back around to face us. The other ranch hands was driftin' out of the barn.

"I can tell ya that I was under General Grant's orders," Pa continued. "I been huntin' a deserter that made off with near fifty thousand dollars in new-minted U.S. Army gold. He was a major in the Grand Army of the Republic and had the trust of Lincoln and Grant. He was supposed to deliver the gold to Washington, but he disappeared on the way from Saint Louis. Grant give me the job of findin' him." Pa stopped a minute and shifted his feet, lookin' at us one by one. "I follered after him west for a spell, but lost his sign at Fort Smith. I figured he was still headin' west, so I come along. I heard he was in Denver. Then I was told he'd come on over here in the valley. I ain't seen him yet, but when I do I figure to take him back."

Danny cleared his throat, "Looks like we're here doing the same thing, Pa. I got the same orders, except mine came at Fort Leavenworth."

Now, that explained a bunch of questions for me all at the same time. It explained how come Danny and his men got out of the Army so easy, and why he'd took an interest in local doin's. He was huntin' him a man and some gold.

"You know this man by sight, Pa?" Dan asked.

"I do. And he knows me, except with no good favor. He was one of Grant's close men, 'til I showed up. Grant kinda shoved him aside when I come into the camp. Told me that Major Dunn was a boot-lickin' simperin' kinda fella and wouldn't tell him things straight out. I reckon Dunn hates me, and I got no cause to love him neither. He tried to have me killed a time or two back in the territory." Pa paused for a minute, rubbed his hand over his face, and looked up at us boys. "I did make a trip back to the farm," he said. "It was near a year after the war ended. Accordin' to the neighbors, I was 'bout three days late on catchin' Matt 'fore he left for Kansas." He sighed and his face took on a sad-dog expression that made him look ten years older. "I was under orders and had to get back to Washington, so I couldn't trace Matthew out. I reckoned me and Ma had raised him right, and he was older than I was when I took out, so I trusted on him to make his own way." He stopped a second and looked off toward the loft and then back to us. "I said good-bye to Ma under the oak tree and headed back east."

He shifted his rifle to his other hand, and I took notice. It was a Winchester '66 with a bunch of fancy work on it, both stock and receiver. It was as beautiful a piece of work as I'd ever seen.

He turned back and looked me up and down. I reckoned he was seein' an oversize farm boy that needed a shave and a haircut.

"From what I seen so far, Matt's done all I figured him for and more," Pa said, talkin' to the other boys. "I knew when I left and told him to round all of you up when the war ended, he'd get it done if it could be." He looked me up and down again. "You done right well, Matthew, and you become a fine figure of a man."

I felt a giant lump comin' up in my throat. This was actually my father, and the whole family, 'cept Ma, was back together again. I was feelin' kinda edgy with everyone lookin' at me, so I turned and walked over to the Morgan I'd rode off the mountain.

"Matt, you don't get off too far. I want to have a talk with ya," Pa said. I nodded, and he, Dan, Mike, and Owen continued talking.

I walked the Morgan gelding toward the far end of the barn.

He was a beautiful animal, and I'd used him hard. I figured he was mine now, since the feller that had been sittin' on him didn't have much use for him. I put him in a stall next to Sin, grabbed up a piece of sackin', and rubbed him down all over. You could tell that the man that'd owned him had taken pride in him, and the chestnut-colored horse was used to bein' handled. He had near as good manners as Sin. I spent some time on the Morgan and then on Sin. I rubbed 'em down all over good then fussed over their legs. Horses ain't much different than people in that they just natural like to have somebody pay attention to 'em.

"They look good, Matt."

I stopped workin' on the horses and looked over to Pa as he walked up. My brothers had left the barn, probably for bed, and we were alone. "I didn't hug on ya, boy, 'cause I didn't know if you'd stand for it," he said. "I know you took a blood oath when Ma was killed, and I know you made good on it. I reckoned you might be havin' some hard feelin's, since I should've been there with you and Ma."

I looked at him, sizin' him up. He weren't as big as I remembered, and he was showin' some miles. He was drawed over some, and I could tell he was in pain from his wound. His eyes were still the same, and he carried the rifle just the way I remembered he carried the Hawken when we was back home. I couldn't find it in me to be mad at him nor spiteful.

"It be done with, Pa," I said. "Me and Ma would've liked to have heard from ya once in a while, but it's water that's already run past. No help for it now."

"No, I reckon you're right," Pa said. He was quiet a minute. "I never learned to write, Matthew, and I was always figurin' on gettin' back quicker than I did. I kept tellin' Grant I needed to go home, and he always asked me to do another week or another month to help him clean things up. Finally, a year had slipped past with me hardly knowin' it."

"It happens," I agreed.

"You seem a mite standoffish, boy, and I surely don't want ya hatin' me."

"I don't hate ya, Pa," I said, and I meant it.

He turned and looked from the barn door out into the darkness toward the mountain. ''It was a close thing up there today, Matthew.'' His voice carried back to me. ''I'd a surely went under if you hadn't been watchin' when them skunks come 'round the bend.'' He turned back toward me and looked down at my Colt. I was still wearin' it high on my belt in the cut-down Cavalry holster that I'd started with.

''You're right handy with that pistol,'' he said.

I didn't say nothin'. I figured I didn't need to.

Pa turned back toward the door and then waved toward the Storm King. ''I first seen this country in '26 when me and my partner come in here for beaver. It was Ute country, and they was mostly friendly to us trappers. Leastways, they was more friendly than the tribes up at the Forks of the Missouri.'' He shifted his rifle a little in his hand and leaned against the door frame. ''I built that little stone cabin up there by the rim in the spring of '27. My partner had went north with Ashley and lost his hair up near Fort Henry. That left me trappin' solo, and I liked the country, so I stayed a spell. I come back in after rendezvous, and then wintered over with the Utes. They took me into the tribe, and I helped feed us all with my Hawken.''

He stood up straight, walked to the open door of the barn not five steps off, and then turned toward me again as if he'd made his mind up about somethin'.

''I ain't only lookin' for a man and government gold, Matthew. When I found out Dunn had come to the valley, I decided to take a side trip over here. I found somethin' years ago when I was up here trappin', but never had the chance to track it out.'' He took a small bag off his wide belt and fished around in it. He pulled somethin' out and tossed it to me. I caught it with my left hand and rolled it around on my palm. It was a gold nugget near as big as half of my thumb and surprisin' heavy for as small as it was.

''That's forty dollars worth right there,'' Pa said. ''I figure there's more where that come from. I'll get the man I'm huntin', sure as the sun comes up tomorrow. When that's done, I plan on findin' the gold on this mountain. The Utes told me stories about the yeller stuff, and I know it's around.''

''I know right where to look, Pa.''

He looked at me kinda surprised, and I told him all that I'd seen up on top of Storm King. He was some excited.

''It's just like the Utes told me, Matthew.'' He stopped a minute and looked me hard in the eye. ''I'd sure be proud if'n you'd ride with me when I go lookin'.''

''You get well, and we'll go take a look at the elephant, Pa,'' I said to him. He smiled big, and then he hugged me. I felt a little like bawlin', but I held her in. He'd called me a man, and it weren't seemly for a man to snivel.

''We promised we'd go cover Uncle John in Denver,'' Dan said, ''and me and Pa got a man to find.'' It was evenin', and we was sittin' in the cabin a week after the fight on the mountain. Wedge, Dan, Mike, and Owen had been singin' the old songs, and we was feelin' right homey. The girls had cooked up a powerful good meal, and it near made me feel like singin' too, 'cept I didn't. I figured there was no call to scare the horses down to the barn.

Uncle John and Holstein Tommy O'Neal had left for Denver before I'd found Pa. We'd told John we'd be along purty quick when he left, and the time had come.

Pa had been down at the creek takin' a mighty cold bath, and I could hear him comin' back to the cabin singin' his ownself. He opened the door and looked a mite sheepish when he seen everybody been listenin'. Hearin' him sing let me know where I'd got my voice.

''We got the hay in, and the cows are all pushed up close in the meadows. I figure the hands can keep 'em from headin' back for the high country. We got no snow to fight yet. I'd say this is as good a time as any to head in.'' Wedge was agreein' with what Dan had said about goin' to Denver.

''We're thinking about taking a family trip into Denver, Pa,'' Mike explained. ''We got some last-minute things to buy 'fore the winter sets in, and we promised Uncle John we'd cover his back.''

''Who'd you say?'' Pa asked, lookin' like a gut-shot coyote.

''Uncle John O'Malley,'' Mike repeated.

We hadn't spoken of Uncle John, nor even thought to tell Pa about him.

''I had me a brother named John,'' Pa said in a quiet voice. ''A long time ago and a fer piece from here.''

''It's the same one, Pa,'' Dan said. ''He's got him some trouble over to Denver.''

''I ain't seen none of that part of my family but maybe twice since I left out,'' Pa said. ''Didn't reckon I ever would again.''

''I don't know how many of them is left, but John's out here. I spent some time with him a few months ago,'' I said. ''Seems like a good man.''

''He was my little brother, nearest me in age. I sorely missed him when I left out.''

''I reckon that's the finishin' vote,'' Wedge said.

''We leave day after tomorrow,'' Dan said with a smile. ''We'll pack the wagons, take the girls with us, and stay in town a week or so. Probably do us all good. Besides, most of my men are ready to muster out, for real this time, and I have to do that from Denver.''

''I could do with a change,'' Mike said.

''I guess if we be goin' to town, I'd best find me a preacher. Jess said she'd have me when I asked a couple of days ago,'' Wedge said.

We all stood and slapped the big man on the back. He'd come a long ways from the ear-rippin', nose-stompin' man I'd known in Kansas. Jessie May and Patty come in from one of the other cabins, and everybody just stood around talkin' and laughin'. I slipped out the door and looked up at the yeller, full moon.

''Harvest moon,'' I said to myself. That's what the folks called the full, November moon back in the farm country. I was feelin' kinda low. I'd been thinkin' about Lee every day, and I was missin' her terrible. No tellin' when I'd see her again, or if I even would.

I jumped a little when I seen some movement out in the meadow by the glow of the moon. I couldn't tell what it was, but it was actin' sneaky. I thought maybe it was a bear or even a cougar comin' in after some of our stock. I crept down and stood in the shadow of the barn. As my eyes got used to the dark, I could see the meadows plain. Whatever it had been, I couldn't see it now. I opened the barn door and checked on my horses. Sin pricked his ears up when he heard me, as did the Morgan. I lit a lantern, then went down and stood by the stalls talkin' quiet to both of 'em.

"Well, seems like I got me an O'Malley here in the barn all by hisself."

The voice came from the direction of the barn door I'd left open behind me, and it didn't sound friendly.

"You take your short gun out easy and drop it on the floor," the man said to me. "I'm in a talkin' mood, but I don't want you tryin' any of your fancy stuff with me."

My back was to him, and I had no choice. I knew durn well that he was holdin' a gun on me, most likely a rifle. He was also standin' in the dark where I was standin' in the light of the lantern. He had me treed. I took the Army out careful and let her slide to the floor.

"You ain't so much," the man said. "If you be Matt, I heard you was a pure terror with a gun."

I heard him take a few steps toward me into the barn.

"I got a man said that if I could notch you, he'd have an extry hundred dollars for me when I got back to town."

"Nathan Kurlow?" I asked.

"Him, and I'd bet that Macon Beck will surely sweeten the pot. He hates you nearly as bad as Kurlow. I been paid two hundred dollars gold to kill any one of the O'Malleys, and five hundred for two. You add Kurlow's and Beck's money on top of that, and I could get rich for doin' what comes natural to me."

I heard him take some more steps deeper into the barn. He was gettin' close to me, but not too close. He was a cautious man and a sure-thing shooter. I was as close to bein' dead as I'd been in quite a spell.

"Turn around, O'Malley. I try to always shoot my man in the front side."

I turned around slow, and he seen the Spanish-made knife in my belt.

"You go ahead and go for that knife. That way I'll feel like I give you a chance," he said.

He was an average-sized man wearin' clothes that hadn't been washed since they'd been new. He had four or five days' growth of dark beard, and his face was greasy. Sweat was drippin' off his chin like he'd run five miles, even though it was not particular warm in the barn.

"You got anything to say, O'Malley?" he asked. I was lookin' for an out, but there just weren't one. He cocked the hammer back on a new Winchester '66, and I knew my time had come. He brought the rifle to his shoulder slow and looked down the sights at me. I could feel the sweat start down my back.

I heard the shot, but didn't feel the shock of it. Maybe that was the way it was when you was kilt outright. I watched the greasy man as he dropped the Winchester and toppled over onto his face. He had a sight of blood runnin' out of him, and he was deader than a side of skinned pork.

"Sorry I took so long, Matt. I had to wait until he cleared the end of the loft floor so I could see him."

I looked up and saw Billy Dean standin' at the edge of the halfloft we'd put in above to carry hay. I was certain glad that I'd brought that boy home from Wyomin' with me. I'd forgot he'd taken to sleepin' in the barn. It was lucky for me, but not so lucky for the dead man.

I heard the family comin' from the cabin, and they come runnin' into the barn all primed with their guns in their hands.

"Billy Dean didn't leave you any," I said as I picked up my Colt and dropped it into my belt holster.

Dan leaned down and turned the greasy man over. I heard a horse come runnin' up outside and figured it was Silva. He'd been watchin' the cows.

"Jared Adams," Dan said. "Last time I saw him he was a

sharpshooter for the Army down at the Richmond standoff. He was a killer even then. Really enjoyed his work.''

Dan felt around in the dead man's pockets and came out with two hundred in new gold. ''I 'spect it's time we started keepin' the gold,'' I said. ''Whoever's payin' it out might as well help us get through the winter.''

''Seems only right,'' Pa agreed. Dan dropped the coins into his pocket and looked at us.

''I got to see me a man,'' I said with my lips tight against my teeth. ''I'm sick of bein' hunted like a rabid dog.''

''Easy, Matt,'' Pa said. ''Think it through.''

''I'm done thinkin', Pa, and I'm done bein' a target. Nathan Kurlow's got to be made to pay the price.''

I put the keeper on my Colt and walked past them out the door. I'd come as near to dyin' as I'd ever been, and it weren't a good feelin'. The next time I might not get so lucky.

''I will ride with you, amigo,'' Christian said as he came into the dark beside me. ''I think you are right. There will be no peace here in the valley until we take the fight to them.''

We were ridin' to Denver the day after tomorrow, and I reckoned that was where I was gonna find Kurlow. The time had come.

Chapter Twelve

We rode into Denver with watchful eyes, and our rifles across our saddles. We had enemies about, and they were surely gunnin' for us. The whole clan, except a few of the hands, had come along with us. The girls had things they wanted to get, and likely it was the last time we'd see a big town 'fore the snow flew.

"Let's go see if The Rainbow City has any pies baked," I said. I had a hunger on me. Travelin' always made me hungry. Come to think on it, so did everything else.

Dan and me walked into the restaurant with Pa stayin' out on the porch. I looked around and was taken back to the last time I'd been in. Lee had been here then.

I sit down at my usual table by the window, and Chris came over and pulled out the chair beside me. Danny sit down across from me. Owen and Mike was sittin' at a table next to us, and as I listened to my brothers talkin' I realized it was good to have my family around me.

I looked out the window as Daniel Briggs's black carriage drove down the street. Briggs was the man that thought he was the big frog in Denver, and had been over to Saguache as well. He'd done nothin' to us, but I felt the hair come up on my neck anyhow.

"I found out what he was about," a voice said from behind us. I turned and saw Uncle John. He'd walked out of the kitchen and was lookin' at the Briggs coach. "He wants the Storm King, and he's made no secret of it the past few weeks here in Denver. He has a big plan to settle all that country with farmers, with him selling the land."

"How does he figure to get it?" Danny asked.

''He's been talking around that the O'Malleys don't have rightful title to the ground. He says he bought the entire spread, plus another hundred thousand acres, from the original Mexican land grant holder.''

''That land was never part of a land grant. We checked it out with the federal court before we ever filed the papers,'' Owen said with some heat in his voice from his table beside us.

''Makes no difference to Briggs. He hired a lawyer from Washington to do the research and file the papers.'' Uncle John walked between the tables and looked us over. He got a grin on his face. ''It's a good feeling to have family around me again. I wished Tirley could see his boys right now.'' It was plain that John didn't know about Pa.

''All he's got to do is walk in from the porch,'' I said around a piece of dried apple pie. John looked funny at us and then went half-walkin' half-runnin' out onto the porch. We could hear them two old boys carryin' on outside, but paid 'em little mind.

''Looks like we got more problems than just Kurlow. Briggs gets a good enough lawyer to challenge our title, we could be in for a court fight,'' Danny said with a stricken look on his face.

''We don't have a penny to hire a lawyer to help us neither,'' Wedge said.

Owen looked a mite thoughtful and glanced to Dan. ''I wonder who Briggs was before he came out here, and where he came from. He seems to have a lot of money, and more than a few connections.''

''The money alone would buy the influence,'' Dan said. He reached into his pocket for the gold coins taken from the dead man in the barn. He laid them out on the table one by one with us lookin' on.

''It's all brand-new money,'' Dan said. ''Hardly a scratch on any of it. The dead man never said that Kurlow gave it to him, only that Kurlow and Beck would pay extra. That means somebody else paid him to kill some O'Malleys.''

''We've seen a lot of new gold money with the people who are standin' against us,'' I said.

"I see your point, Matt," Owen said. "Newly minted gold isn't that common."

" 'Cept for fifty thousand or so of government money that's missing," Dan observed. "I wonder what kinda money Dan Briggs is spending?"

"Pa, John, come in here for a minute," Danny hollered loud enough for 'em to hear out on the porch.

When the two older men were standin' close among us, Dan laid out his ideas.

"I'd like for Pa to get a look at Daniel Briggs," he said. "Might be that Dunn and Briggs are the same man, and nobody out here knows what Dunn looks like 'cept Pa." Dan looked from the window across the street to where the Briggs coach had stopped. I started as I saw a man step down from the rig. It was Nate Kurlow.

"We shut off the money supply, and a bunch of that scum hanging with Kurlow will leave," Owen said.

"Kurlow won't," I said. "He took me cuttin' his face up right personal." I was lookin' right at the man we was talkin' about, and I knew the hate ran deep and long in him.

"Some of his men will stick. I heard he's put together a small army," Wedge commented.

"I found out Briggs is also the individual who's behind my trouble with the railroad," Uncle John said. "I took the liberty of sending certain information to a firm of lawyers that I've worked with before. I've already paid them a retainer. I've sent a wire and asked them to research both the case law and written law with regard to the O'Malley claim to the Storm King. I expect an answer from them next week."

"If Dunn and Briggs are the same man, we may not have to worry about our legal problems. We'll have him in chains," Dan said. "We just need to have Pa get a look at him."

"I'd just as soon walk over there right now, and take a gander," Pa said. There was now another man standing beside Kurlow on the boardwalk across the street lookin' toward The Rainbow City. "Who's that?" Pa asked, pointin' out the window.

I climbed to my feet and took the keeper from my Colt. I laid my hat on with a tug. Trouble was standin' across the street, but it was my trouble, and a job I hadn't finished from Kansas.

Macon Beck was standin', talkin' to Kurlow. Kurlow climbed back in the coach, and I saw Beck reach his hand inside, then pull it back out. I thought I caught the gleam of gold, but it might've just been my imagination. Kurlow, or Briggs if he was in the rig, must've told the driver to get 'cause they left down the street at a purty good clip.

"If there be any more of 'em, keep 'em off my back," I said to the brothers, not takin' my eyes from Beck.

"Who is he, boy?" Pa asked me as I started for the door.

"Name's Macon Beck. He's a brother to the man that killed Ma."

"You stand. This is my job." I looked at Pa and seen flint in his eyes. I was some surprised. "You figure this here Beck was with his brother when they killed your Ma and burnt our place?" he asked me.

"I don't know. I guess he might've been."

"Close enough. You filled your blood oath, but I still ain't." He raised the sleeve on his buckskin jacket, and there was a large, angry, red scar on his forearm that was nearly the twin of the one I had. Pa had sworn a blood oath, just as I had, and it was something we Irish took serious. A man either filled the oath or died tryin'. "He's mine," Pa said, "and if I can't cut it, then he falls to you."

"Pa . . ." Danny started to say. Pa turned a look on him that would've froze spit. Weren't none of us gonna argue with Pa.

Pa had taken to carryin' a Colt like mine, a .44, but he kept his bowie and tomahawk still in his belt. He was a hard-lookin' man for all his years, or maybe because of 'em. He stepped out the door and walked to the edge of the boardwalk on our side. "What ya want, Beck?" he hollered over at the big man.

"I want Matt O'Malley. He used his knife on me in Kansas, killed my brother out in the short grass, and made my life hell. I got nothin' to do with you, old man. Just send Matt out, so I can kill 'im."

"You got to walk across me, Beck. You had a hand in killin'

my wife and burnin' my place with your brother. I figure to even the score.''

"Well, if that's what you want," Beck yelled. He drew his pistol while he was talkin' and come up shootin'. Pa started walkin' toward him without even takin' his pistol from his belt. Beck was shootin' too quick, and the range was too far for good shootin' with a short gun. A window broke in The Rainbow City as a wild shot hit, and the patrons dove for the floor. I stood up and watched Pa as he kept on walkin'.

Beck was startin' to panic, 'cause Pa was gettin' too close. He emptied his pistol and dropped the cylinder out diggin' for a new one on his belt. Pa kept walkin' as Beck fumbled to reload. Pa was close, maybe thirty feet, when he stopped. He drew his tomahawk from his belt just as Beck raised his pistol to shoot again. There was no way Beck was gonna miss at that range.

Pa flung the 'hawk just as Beck shot. I saw Pa flinch, and the war ax made a lazy turn in the air. I heard the thunk as it hit Beck right in the middle of the forehead, and the big man fell over onto his back.

Pa stood a minute, and then walked to where Beck lay. It was over and done, and a chapter in my life closed as Macon Beck's blood seeped into the dust of Denver City.

We went runnin' out as Pa retrieved his 'hawk. "You okay?" I yelled as we hit the boardwalk. Pa turned and waved his arm, then come walkin' across the street toward us.

"He nicked me up a little, but nothin' to count," he said. When he got to us Patty lifted his shirt and looked at the bullet furrow along his ribs. It was seepin' a little blood, so she took him into the café to fix him up.

I looked down the street and felt the fire start in me. I'd seen Kurlow with Beck, and then Beck come for me. It didn't take a lot of book learnin' to figure that Kurlow was at the bottom of my troubles, and maybe Briggs as well, but surely Kurlow.

I turned and started to walk up the street toward the Golden Slipper Saloon. It was owned by Kurlow and it was where he hung out with his cronies.

"Where you goin', Matt?" Dan asked.

"I got me some business up the street," I said. My voice was tight and my jaw clenched.

"Not alone, *señor*," Chris said. "It is what they want."

"He's right, Matt. Divide and conquer," Danny said.

"You can come along, if you're a mind. Just don't get in front of me."

I walked up the street with Danny and Chris close beside me. Chris was carrying the double ten gauge, and Dan had slipped the keeper from his pistol.

I stepped through the batwing doors of the saloon and stepped quickly to one side. The interior was dark after the bright light of the cold sun outside. It took a minute of blinkin' my eyes for me to get accustomed. We walked up to the bar watchin' close about and waitin' for trouble to come upon us. I was ready.

"What can I do fer ya?" The bartender had a surly attitude.

"A small piece of information," Danny replied in an even tone before I could speak. "Can you tell us where Nathan Kurlow could be found?"

The barkeeper batted his eyes and swallered. "Most often if you want to talk to Kurlow you just leave word with me, and I'll let him know."

"I don't want to just find him. I plan on killin' him," I said with my jaws all bunched up tight.

"If you be huntin' Nathan Kurlow, he'll find you first," the bartender said with a smirk on his face. That tore it for me. I reached across the bar sudden-like and grabbed the dirty man by the front of the shirt. I drug him across the bar and threw him to the floor. He hit with a sizable noise and the wind was driven out of him.

"Stand easy, amigos," I heard Chris say. I looked over, and he had the shotgun pointed at a trio of men that had risen from a nearby table.

"Barkeep, if I was you, I'd make with the talkin'," I said. "I plan on having a conversation with Kurlow, or, if he wants, a shooting war. I've gotten to where I don't care much which it is."

"I hear ya talkin', but I don't see any of your graveyards," a bearded man said from the opposite side of the room. He'd been sittin' at a table by hisself, and he had the look of a tough man. There wasn't a mite of fear on him. I looked over and Chris was still holdin' the shotgun steady on the three that had stood up. Dan had stepped to the far end of the bar where he could see the whole room, and he had his hand on his gun. Weren't nobody gonna interfere with what was comin' next.

I took a long step toward the bearded man, and I could see the light come up in his eyes.

"I ain't carryin' a gun, O'Malley. It's over to the gunsmith's." He held his arms out from his sides to show me. I took my Colt off and laid it on a table, then followed it with my knife. The bearded man had a crooked smile on his face as he slipped out of his coat.

I was young, with little experience, and this man was older and bigger than me by twenty pounds. He had a gut hangin' over his belt, but it weren't much fat. On the other hand, I'd been hayin', cuttin' firewood, wrestling cows, and doin' all manner of other work. I was hard as stone, and huntin' in the high country had helped my air. I felt good, and I planned on takin' the fight to Kurlow and his men startin' right here.

The bearded man took a step toward me, then come in a runnin' rush. I'd been expecting such a thing and sidestepped him just as he got to me. He bowled over a table and lit on his face. I took a step back from him to give him room to get up, knowin' he'd have given me no such chance.

He swung a big right hand at my face, and I ducked under it. I nailed him with a right cross to the chin, and he blinked his eyes, but kept comin'. I hit him in the ribs and moved back from him a step. He rocked me with a left I hadn't seen, and I tasted blood in my mouth.

He hit me again, and then kicked out at me. He missed, but I jumped back so fast I fell over a chair. He come at me with feet, boots, and spurs. I stuck my leg up to deflect him, then rolled onto my side and jumped to my feet. Just as I got stood, he nailed me with a right and left combination that put me on my back again. He flung a table out of the way and come at me with a roar. I rolled again and made him miss. I got to my knees, and then my feet in one fluid motion. I wasn't hurt, but I was some surprised. The man could fight, he was fast, and he could hit.

I circled 'round him, then he come at me again. I stood my ground and nailed him with a quick jab in the mouth followed by a straight shot into his paunch. It hurt him. I could see it in his eyes. I was sweatin' like a fevered pig, and there was blood drippin' from my face onto the floor. I was warmed up and feelin' fit. Then the fury started crawlin' up from my gut. I knew better than to fight mad 'cause it blinds ya, but I meant to show all of 'em a thing or two about what we O'Malleys brung to the table.

He rushed toward me with his hands up, showin' he'd learned a thing or two about fightin' somewhere. I didn't wait on him. I took a quick step toward him, knocked his hands down, and hit him as hard as I could with my right hand. It sounded just like a double-jack hittin' rock. He stepped back, and I hit him again, hard, right on the point of the chin. The jolt moved him back again, and I followed fast.

There weren't no mercy in me, and what happened was just plain ugly. I give him a beatin', I surely did. Every time he'd try to fall, I'd hold him up and smash at his face and body with my fists. I kept it up until I was blowin' like a steam vent. I stepped back from him, and he fell onto his face. I turned back to the room and saw another man lookin' a mite froggy. I jumped toward him, and he run out the door with me screamin' right on his heels. He was a fast man on his feet, and I was winded, so I didn't catch him.

I turned back into the saloon and quick stepped over to the three men that Chris had kept off me. They was surely Kurlow men, and I didn't like the look on their faces. I hit the tallest one as hard as I could, and he just weren't expectin' it. He laid out on his back colder than the north wind in January.

I lost it then. I was seein' through a veil of red, and I broke everything in the saloon that could be broke. I raged, yelled, caterwauled, howled, screamed, and made a terrible mess of the place. I broke every bottle, table, chair, mirror, window, and glass I could find. I even ripped the back door off the hinges. I finally wore myself out and turned toward Chris and Dan. Their eyes was big as saucers. I walked over to where the barkeep was sittin' on the floor, and hauled him to his feet.

"You tell Nate Kurlow that I'm here for him, and I ain't leavin' 'til I find him," I said. My voice was shakin', and I sorely needed a drink of water. I grabbed the bartender with my other hand as well, and I flung him. He flew through the air and hit the side of the saloon so hard that he broke the studding and crashed through the wall, landin' outside in the alley.

The bearded man was movin' a little and groanin', so I knew he weren't dead, and I was right proud of myself. I'd laid out three men, literally destroyed a place of business, and hadn't killed nary a person.

Chapter Thirteen

We went back to The Rainbow City, and I sat down on the boardwalk. I was fair tuckered out. I looked down the street and saw a familiar figure walkin' toward us.

"If I ain't mistakin', that looks like Shadrach Taylor comin', and I'd almost guess that he ain't happy with the O'Malleys," I said.

"It's likely," Dan agreed. "We haven't been in town but a few hours and we've beat the stuffin's out of folks, destroyed a place of business, and killed a man."

"We have been a mite busy, ain't we?" I asked, and smiled up at Danny.

"What the heck have you boys been up to?" Shad asked as he got close. He weren't smilin'.

"We're just gonna head home, Marshal. We stopped in for some pie," Wedge said in a serious voice.

"You're not heading anywhere until I say you can. And I'm not a marshal, I'm a deputy sheriff," Shad said. He was vexed, and with reason. I didn't blame him.

He ran his hand over his face and looked over at Beck's body still layin' in the street. "Who did for the loudmouth?" he asked.

"My pa," I said, "but Beck was huntin' me. I killed his brother a while back."

Pa come walkin' out and looked at the badge on Shad's shirt.

"I reckon I'm the man you want, Sheriff," Pa said.

"Tell me what happened," Shad said.

"That Beck feller was with the gang that killed my wife and burnt my place back East. He's been doggin' Matt for quite a spell, and Matt was gonna walk across the street and do fer him.

142

I told Matt it was my job, and if I couldn't handle Beck, then he could have him. I handled him.''

''We'll set an inquest for three this afternoon. I need everybody there,'' Shad said. He turned and walked across the street.

Come three o'clock we all gathered at the courthouse and told our stories. The jury at the inquest listened to our testimony and voted that Beck had been askin' for what he got. They ruled it was a legal killin'. We left the courthouse and walked back toward the Rainbow. Holstein Tom O'Neal come out of an alley and joined us as we walked.

''Nathan Kurlow left town riding north an hour ago. The good Irish lass that told me of this said he had thirty men with him. They all had packhorses.''

We stopped walkin' to listen.

''Any word on where they were heading, or why they left?'' Uncle John asked.

''The word is around town that Kurlow felt the breath of the banshee. He got news delivered by a whisper of the wind that Shadrach Taylor's two U.S. Marshal brothers were coming here. It is said that they have a warrant for him on suspicion of murder. There is also the hint that he had a hand in stealing over a hundred new rifles from a shipment headed for Fort Leavenworth a few months ago,'' Tommy said.

''Let us know if you hear where Kurlow might be going. As long as he's alive and free, we are all in danger,'' John said. Tommy nodded and walked back toward the alley. He stopped short and looked right at me. ''Kurlow did do one thing before he left, laddie. He said that you would not live to see the summer grass grow tall.'' With them encouraging words, Tommy disappeared into the alley.

We continued our walk toward the Rainbow, silent now, thinking about what we'd just heard. As we approached the café, Meshach Taylor, U.S. Marshal, stepped from the door, and beside him was a man that had the look of the other Taylor boys. He was wearin' a U.S. Marshal's badge on his vest.

''I can't believe I had to pay for my own meal,'' Meshach said with a grin, stickin' his hand out. ''How are you, Matt?''

"I'm doin' good," I replied, returning his smile and shaking his hand. "If I was to guess I'd say this was the third Taylor boy," I said, noddin' my head toward the man with Meshach.

"Actually, our mom figured me for number one. She likes me better than the other two," Abendigo said with a smile.

"You're lookin' at Abendigo Taylor," Meshach said. "We're lookin' for Kurlow," Meshach added. "Abendigo was given the arrest papers by the same judge that swore him in. The judge sent me a telegram at Kansas City and told me to team up with Abendigo."

"We've got a warrant to serve, and I think we're going to need all the help we can get," Abendigo added.

"You're gonna have to go on the hunt. We just heard that Kurlow and his gang left out, goin' north," I said.

Meshach's face became serious. "I heard that as well, but I also have information he plans on pointing back south after he's well away from town." Meshach's right hand dropped unconsciously to the butt of his Colt, and he looked down the street. "He's got a band of renegade Indians wintering over somewhere down there. If you add the men he picked up here, he probably has a bigger force with him than the Army has at Fort Lewis."

"I hope he leaves the country," Owen said. "We've had enough trouble this year."

"If he doesn't leave, I can promise you he'll be in jail," Meshach said, lookin' over at his brother. "We're going to get an Army detachment and go after him."

"Well, good huntin', and keep your head down. Me and Kurlow have been at each other a couple of times, and he ain't gonna be easy," I said.

"No, we didn't expect he would be." Meshach looked down the street again, and a smile split his face. "Look who's comin'."

We all looked and saw Shadrach walkin' up to us from the direction of the jail. It took him a few minutes to pull even with us. He looked like a kid who just ate the last cookie in the jar, so his sister couldn't have it. One of them self-satisfied looks.

"Who died and left you money?" Abendigo asked.

"I got appointed sheriff right after we got done with the inquest."

"You what?" Meshach asked.

"I did," Shad said. "Seems the elected sheriff, my boss, was being paid off by Kurlow. I've often wondered since him and Kurlow seemed pretty thick, but I didn't have any proof. I told my friend, Tom Kelshaw, the town marshal, what I thought, and he started watching the sheriff. Seems he saw the sheriff right in the act of taking some gold money. It wasn't just the marshal saw it. Two of the marshal's men, and Byers, the newspaper guy, saw it as well. They went to the county commission this morning, and now the former sheriff is sitting in his own jail."

"Congratulations, Sheriff," I said, and stuck out my hand. We all shook his hand, and then Shad and his two brothers turned and walked back off toward the courthouse.

We watched the three men a moment as they walked away. "Those are the kind of men that will civilize the West," Uncle John said.

He was right. Good solid men that knew right from wrong and had respect for the law of the land. They was the kind of men that would put their lives on the line to stand between the lawless and the good folks. I greatly admired them. I was also downright glad we could count 'em as friends.

We went into the Rainbow and ordered coffee. I relaxed a bit and listened to the easy conversation of my friends and family. There was a lull in the talkin', and Owen's chair scraped on the pine-board floor.

"It's been a big day. I think I'll find Patty, and go to the library," Owen said.

Uncle John stood as well. "I have to send some telegrams, and I need to meet with a couple of engineers yet this afternoon."

We began to break up into singles and little groups, each goin' his own way. Chris, Pa, and me headed for the livery to check the stock. We kept our eyes peeled, knowin' there were folks about that had no love for us, though I couldn't for the life of me figure out why. We was some of the most lovable people that ever been put on God's earth.

* * *

We spent most of a slow week, doin' mostly nothin'. We went to a play one evenin' that Owen and Uncle John plainly enjoyed. As we was walkin' out of the opera house, Pa slid up beside me. "You understand what was goin' on in there, Matthew?" he asked me.

I felt purty superior 'cause I had really took hold and got the meat of the story. I reckoned it was up to me to explain stuff to Pa, since he didn't have my refinin'.

"There was this fella name Mark, and this lady named Cleo. She lived in a place called Alexandria where there was quite a bit of gypsy lust." I'd caught that gypsy lust part right at the beginnin' of the show, and it stuck with me.

"I knew it," Pa exploded. "I couldn't understand what they was sayin', but I knew it weren't the kind of show that Ma would've wanted me takin' her boys to. Gypsy lust." Pa was some disgusted, and I thought maybe I ought to move him off the gypsies down to the main part of the play. We was walkin' down the street in a bunch, not payin' much mind to those around us.

"John O'Malley!" The voice rang strong and clear against the quiet talkin'. It come from the shadows of a side street. We pulled up short, and I stepped up even with Uncle John. I took the keeper from my Colt. Mike stepped up beside me. He had his hand on the special Greener shotgun he'd made that he carried on a sling under his coat. He carried deershot in it, and it was pure deadly at the range we was standin'.

"We want no one else," the voice said, "except John O'Malley."

"You take Uncle John, you get us all," Danny said in a voice that carried through the crisp night air.

"Step out where I can see you," Uncle John said.

Four men stepped out from the shadows and faced us square. They had the look of Texas boys, and their guns was slung down low on separate belts with holsters. It didn't look all that handy to me.

"What can I do for you gentlemen?" John asked in a voice most pleasant.

"Man we work for wants you dead, O'Malley."

"I appreciate a man that gets straight to the heart of the problem," John replied.

'Bout this time, had it been me, I'd have cut my dog loose and been tryin' to shorten the odds some. It weren't my play. It was Uncle John's, and I'd let him call the tune.

"Did you hear that, Sheriff Taylor?" Uncle John asked in a loud voice.

"I did, Mr. O'Malley. It seems these individuals have it on their mind to disrupt the peace and quiet of my city." Shad's voice came from behind the killers and off to the right.

"Darn it, Sheriff. How many times I got to tell you that the city is mine. You got the county," another voice came from the other side of the street, but still behind the killers.

"Oh, sorry. I keep forgetting, Marshal," Shad said in a conversational tone. "John, if you and the rest of your clan want to shoot these gents, you go right ahead. We'll clean up what you don't take care of."

It looked to me that the Texas boys weren't as anxious to shoot Uncle John as they had been at first. Their hands moved away from their short guns, and they was lookin' kinda sick.

"What will it be, gentlemen? If you try for me, you have all the O'Malleys to deal with. I couldn't talk them out of it if I tried," John said, lookin' right at the man that was the talker. "You have a choice. You can die, or you can go to jail."

I thought he was gonna try it. I surely did. He tensed for a minute, and he looked at John with hate-filled eyes. He was bent over a little at the waist, and his hand was fair tremblin' he wanted to go for it so bad. His mind wanted to go for it, but his body knew that it was gonna have a bunch of holes punched in it.

"Cleve, give it up," one of his buddies said.

"Drop your guns on the ground, and get your hands up where I can see them," Shad said in a strong voice.

The Texas boys did as they was told, and the lawmen walked

out where we could see 'em. The killers was right lucky they'd showed some sense. The three Taylor boys walked over from the right side of the street, and Tom Kelshaw, the town marshal, with three of his deputies come from the other side. The town boys all had shotguns.

"We'll take charge of them from here," Shad said.

"Thank you, Sheriff," Uncle John said. "Marshal." Uncle John touched his hat brim to the lawmen. They walked the prisoners toward the county jail.

"Close," Wedge said. His voice made us all feel like we'd just let out a breath we'd been holdin'.

"I saw all the badges when we came from the play," John explained. "I also noticed that they kept pace with us as we walked, but out of sight. I assumed something was up." Uncle John turned and looked at us one by one. "I guess I don't need to tell you all how much I appreciate . . ." he started to say. His voice broke.

Pa walked up to him and clapped him on the back. "Let's go get some pie."

Mornin' came bright, but cold. There'd been a ring around the moon the night before, and Pa figured us for a storm. We was drinkin' coffee and eatin' our breakfast. We'd sold the Rainbow to the cook a few days before, and he was a happy man. He'd kept us in pie for a week, not to mention an occasional batch of sugar-dipped bear sign that lasted no time at all. He'd paid us a fair price, and everyone come out a winner. We'd given the money to Owen for keepin'. We figured to give a good portion to Lee, if we ever heard from her again. Sellin' The Rainbow City seemed like cutting the last string I had that held her to me.

"I think it's time we went home," Owen said in a quiet voice. Nobody said anything, but we all knew he was right. Kurlow was gone, the ranch was being tended by just a handful of men, and there was work waitin' on us. If Kurlow decided to move against the ranch while we was gone, we'd lose everything we'd worked for.

I sit at a table lookin' out at the street, drinkin' coffee and thinkin'. Owen had said it was time to go home, and it struck me that we all thought of the Storm King as home now. We'd fought shoulder to shoulder, worked from sunup to dark, had friends and people we loved that died defending the place, and we'd all come together at the Storm King. Maybe that was the most of it. We were together for the first time in many years as family. I looked around me at the people that was most important in my life. Pa and Uncle John were laughin' at some story Pa had told. Wedge, Patty, Owen, and Jessie were all sitting at one table, talking quiet about their hopes and dreams. Danny and Mike was drinking coffee and watchin' the servin' girl who was battin' her eyes at 'em. Me and Chris were sittin' at our normal table, not talkin' but knowin' that the other was close. It was a good feeling bein' here with these folks. There was only one thing missin'.

I missed Lee more than ever I'd thought I could. She was the corner post of what I'd made my plans around. With her gone, I knew I'd drawn in some, and I had a fear on me that I was gettin' mean and low-down. I knew that the Storm King was my home, but it weren't my future. Not without Lee. There was a restlessness on me, and it was drivin' me. I'd probably stick 'til spring, but after the grass started greenin' up enough for travel feed, I was headin' out. I'd made up my mind.

"I'm goin'," I said aloud, not really meanin' to.

"When you do, *señor,* I shall ride with you. We are like the beans in a pod. We are alike. I need to see things and to learn," Chris said across the table to me. He smiled that brilliant smile of his and took a sip from his cup. I just nodded, not trustin' my voice.

Pa stood and come walkin' over. "I don't mind winterin' over in a place, but come spring I reckon we ought to go find the elephant." He leaned down and looked at me straight on. "I got a job to finish for the government, and then I'm free of 'em. I got a place I want to show you west of the San Juans, and then maybe we'll ride on over to the canyon country."

Holstein Tommy come walkin' in, and we turned to look at him. "Daniel Briggs left town early this morning. The livery man says he was speaking of the golden land and warm sun of California. The Texas men confessed to the sheriff that Briggs was the one that paid them to kill Jonathan.''

''Darn,'' Dan said. ''We should've moved faster.''

''No help for it now, Son,'' Pa said. ''I figure it ain't gonna take both of us to round him up anyhow.''

''No, now that we got a line on him it ought to be a little easier,'' Dan agreed. ''If he's our man, and I'd say the chances are pretty good he is.'' He stood and walked over to the window by our table. ''I always thought it was a little strange that you and I ended up with near the same orders anyhow. They sent two O'Malleys to get the same man. That don't seem like coincidence to me.''

Pa snorted a laugh. ''You don't know Grant like I do. I can promise ya it weren't done by accident. He probably figured that two O'Malleys would be that much worse for Major Dunn.'' Pa stopped and looked out onto the street. There was a light breeze blowin' from the north, and it held the promise of new snow.

Pa turned and looked at us again. ''Only thing that makes me a mite unhappy about the whole thing is that Grant didn't tell me he was puttin' you on it, Danny. I didn't know where you boys was. If'n he'd've told me, my mind would have rested easier.''

''Maybe he didn't know, Pa. You know how the Army is. I got my orders at Leavenworth. They might have just said to put somebody on it, and I was the closest.''

''You believe that?'' Pa asked.

''No,'' Dan replied with a smile.

Pa smiled and drained his cup. ''Let's get packed and get goin' '' Pa said. ''I'm a mite worried about the ranch.''

''I paid off all my men except Tommy,'' Uncle John said. ''I also got confirmation on my contracts this morning by telegraph.'' Patty started clappin', and we all joined in. Uncle John beamed, and then held up his hands. ''I learned as well that not only is the O'Malley claim on the Storm King valid, but it is now patented,'' he said. ''My attorneys have requested an indictment for fraud against Daniel Briggs to go along with the charges of attempted murder here. He's in a world of trouble.''

"We catch up to him, he's gonna spend the rest of his life in a cell," Danny said.

"We'll catch up to him," Pa said. I looked over at him and was glad I wasn't in Briggs's shoes.

"I have one more request," John said. "I'd like to come out to the ranch." He looked kinda embarrassed as he said it. "As you know, my resources are tied up with this railroad venture. I, or I should say we, won't start seeing any money for about a year. I, ah, well . . . I seem to be temporarily without funds."

Pa laughed and slapped Uncle John on the back. "You mean you're broke."

"Not broke, but I will have to sell some properties back East to tide me over. In the meantime . . ."

"We can't have an O'Malley living here in rags and soaking off the good will of the county," Owen said.

"Get your geegaws together and let's get goin'," Pa said.

That got us started movin', and in an hour we were headin' down the street lookin' toward the south.

We'd been ridin' some hours when Pa rode up beside me. We was stirrup to stirrup, and it appeared he had somethin' on his mind.

"How many men you killed, boy?" he asked me flat out.

His question took me by surprise, and I thought on it a while.

"I don't rightly know, Pa. Too many."

"I'm glad to hear ya say that, Matthew. You're good with that short gun and faster gettin' into action than anybody I ever seen. You might be too good."

"You ain't the first person to say that. I try to be careful, but it seems I never have a choice. I don't like bein' pushed, and I ain't much on backin' down."

"I wouldn't have it any other way, boy, but you got to be watchful." He fell quiet for a minute, and we listened to our horses walking on the hard-packed trail. "When I was a young-ster, maybe a year or two older than you are now, I killed a man that was a friend to me. He'd fished my biscuits out of the fire back up in the Three Forks country, and I was beholden to him. We'd rode together for a year, trappin', fightin' the Blackfeet, and nearly starvin' to death. We come into rendezvous, and he drank most of a jug of lightnin' by hisself. He was a mean drunk, and he hit near anybody that was still standin'. I weren't a drinker and stayed out of his line, hopin' he wouldn't get it in his mind that he needed to whip on me.'' Pa cleared his throat, took his hat off, and slicked his hair back with his hand, then put his hat back on careful. He was having trouble with the tellin' of the story, and I bided my time.

''He found a Crow woman somewheres back in the Aspens,'' Pa continued, ''and he come draggin' her out into the firelight. She was a likely lookin' gal, young, and scared. She was cryin', and he threw her around some. Nobody else would say nothin' to him, being mean drunk that way, and they started to lookin' my direction. I was his partner. I guess they figured I should stop him. Fact was, I felt like I should too. I stepped out into the light and called his name. He turned on me with his big skinner in his hand. The girl ran away, and that made him madder yet. He come for me. I fought him off for a spell, but he nicked me up some. I tried to get away from him, but he wouldn't allow it. Finally, my O'Malley temper come on me along with my pride. I stuck him with my Green River, deep and long. He called my name out twice as he died.'' Pa stopped a minute and looked at the mountains close on our west side. Then he looked right at me. There was tears standin' in his eyes, not fallin', but there just the same.

''I've never been able to shake his voice out of my head,'' he said in near a whisper. ''I can still hear him callin' my name. I can still see his face.''

''He pushed it on you,'' I said.

''He did that, but if I'd a kept my head, he'd still be alive.''

Pa shut up, and then kicked his horse lightly in the ribs and caught up with Danny. I knew what he was sayin'. I'd had the feelin', maybe the fear, that the same thing could happen to me. There was dead men on my back trail, and weren't a one of 'em didn't need killin', but I knew what Pa was sayin'. My temper and my speed with a short gun might be a bad combination.

The wind hit us a blast from the north, and there were tiny

grains of snow in it that felt like sand on the back of my neck. We was due for snow, and it looked like it was about to catch up to us.

We wintered over purty well, losing only a handful of stock to the weather and critters. Jessie May and Wedge had got married on Christmas day. Most of the town of Saguache had come out to the ranch for the doin's, and Otto Mears done the marryin'. Chief Ouray come in after a big blizzard in February and told us his people was near starved out. We cut him out ten head of young steers and rode with him back to his camp. The band was glad to see us, and we helped them butcher. The Utes had a deserved reputation of bein' mean folks that kept mostly to themselves. Out of all the Injuns, the Utes was only a half-step behind the Blackfeet for hatin' white men. We'd got along with 'em well enough, but we was the exception. They was gettin' edgy about more people comin' into their land. We mostly held with the same notion that the Mormons had. Brigham Young had told his saints that it was better to feed the Injuns than to fight with 'em. Saved the Mormons some trouble, and we surely hoped it'd work for us.

Ignacio had moved his band clear west, according to Ouray. Ignacio had all the pushin' he could stand, and taken out. They said he was over toward the canyon country near the Sleepin' Ute Mountain.

We'd heard some of Kurlow and his crowd from time to time. They stopped a train on the main line east of Cheyenne, robbed a stage up near the Greely Station, shot an Army paymaster and stole over three thousand dollars, run off a bunch of horses at Trinidad, and had three or four shootin' scrapes. Looked to me that Kurlow had thrown off any sign of respectability and had become an out-and-out desperado. I hoped the Army or the Taylor boys would catch up to him before he'd ever get around to us at the Storm King. One thing I'd done was to start carryin' two short guns. I had my regular Colt in the holster and another stuck in my belt close by my hand. I reckoned that if they caught me somewhere, I could leastways make 'em dodge twelve shots before I had to change cylinders. I also took notice that Chris never let me out of his sight. It was almost embarrassin' the way he stuck by me, but it was a good feelin' as well.

We got a March thaw, and then another week of hard freeze, but I could smell spring in the air. Come the first part of April, the grass was greenin', and we had over a hundred new-dropped calves. Our heifers was havin' trouble, but the older cows shucked calves like there was nothin' to it. Jess and Patty had three or four calves they was feedin' in the cabins that was too weak to feed themselves, and the mother cows hung close to the door, makin' a bother of themselves. It was shapin' up to be a fair season, but I still had it on my mind to leave out.

I'd done a sight of thinkin' on the matter, and it seemed to me that if I left the ranch, and Kurlow still wanted me, I'd at least take the fight away from the ranch. If I stayed at the ranch, he'd surely come against us again, and we'd already paid a high price in lives. I didn't want to see any more of my friends and family laid out on the hill under the pine tree. Kurlow had made his brag, and I knew he'd try to make good on it before the summer was well along. I reckoned that this time we was gonna meet at a place I picked, and we was gonna finish it. When we met again, one of us was gonna die.

Chapter Fourteen

There was a warm breeze blowin' down from the Storm King, and I could smell the tall pines. It weren't light yet, but there was pink showin' along the east edge of the sky. Sin stamped his foot as I strapped the saddlebags on behind the saddle. The Morgan still had his head in the feed bunk where I'd laid out a bait of oats for him. He had panniers on. I had the canvas packs already loaded and ready to sling over the panniers.

"What ya think we'll find?" Pa asked me, his voice quiet, but still loud in the nearly silent barn.

"I don't know, Pa. I didn't look that close when I was up there. I found a cave, but it looked like it was where they was shelterin'. I'd think there might be a shaft somewheres."

"Never can tell about them old Spanish boys. They might just have found an outcrop of quartz and dug 'til it was gone."

"Might've," I agreed. "Still, it gives us an excuse to go riding the country."

"As if we need much of an excuse." Pa smiled over his saddle at me.

We'd decided to ride up to the top of Storm King and take a look at the old Spanish mine workin's. I had it in my mind that there might still be some gold up there since the Spanish hadn't taken it with them. Their skeletons in the cave made me figure they was killed before they had a chance to get all the gold out.

I had my Henry rifle in the saddle boot, and I noticed that Pa had left the fancy new Winchester up at the main cabin. He was packin' a Spencer in .56 caliber. It carried seven shots and had the wallop of a mad bull buffalo. It hurt the shooter near as bad as whatever was shot 'cause of the recoil. I was still carryin' the

two pistols, and I noticed that Pa had his old Colt's Dragoon in
a saddle holster near the horn, plus his .44 in his belt. If trouble
come to us on the mountain, we'd at least make a little noise.

Pa swung up in the saddle and grabbed the tie rope of his
packhorse. "Let's get goin', boy," he said. "I've sat so long in
one place I got moss growin' on me."

We had nearly a hundred head of calves that we was holdin'
up close to the barn in a big corral we'd built. There was a grizz
recently moved into our meadows, probably from the San Juans,
and we'd lost a few calves to him. We couldn't afford to lose
any, so we'd penned them closer to the buildin's. The big bear
hadn't returned since we'd made the gather, and it was our hope
maybe he'd move on down the valley.

I grabbed the lead rope to the Morgan and climbed into my
saddle. Sin looked over his shoulder at me like he was disgusted.
He'd been ready to go a long time ago.

We rode out through the open doors and made our way across
the meadow to the creek. Pa stopped and looked toward the south.
"Why don't we go back up the way that Chris and me come
down after the fight?" he asked. "I doubt if anybody is watchin'
us, but might not hurt to have a caution."

"Sounds good to me," I replied. Pa had told me once that
gold was a thing hard found and even harder to keep. If there
was any shafts or seams on top that we could work, there was
no sense markin' a trail straight up to it. It'd take us longer goin'
around the mountain, but time wasn't serious to us right now
anyhow.

We rode through the meadows, and I looked to the east. It'd
gotten to be a habit with me. Lee was always on my mind, but
we hadn't heard a thing from her. I figured by now she'd found
herself a city gent that would take good care of her. Every time
I thought of her with another man, I got this big lump in my
throat. I surely missed her.

I still had it on my mind to leave, but I didn't want to leave
the ranch without I had contributed somethin' to the project. All
I had to offer right now was my strong back and arms. If we
found some gold, we could move on and feel like we'd done our

part to keep things goin'. Me, Pa, and Chris had made our plans, but we just didn't feel right 'til we could provide help for the partnership.

We rode for near two hours south and then south by west. We broke out of some trees and were fair surprised to see a group of wagons down in a meadow with folks standin' about. As we rode closer, I realized they was more than just wagons. They was painted in all kinds of colors and had canvases rolled out that made shades. There was folks in fancy clothes sittin' in chairs under the canvas apparently eatin'. It was too late for breakfast and it was early for noonin'. I couldn't figure what they was doin'.

"Howdy," a man said as we rode up. "Light and sit." The man that spoke was medium sized, and his face was seamed with age. He was no tenderfoot, and his rifle was close to hand. The fancy folks smiled at us, and as I looked 'em over, I realized they was foreign. Now, I ain't just talkin' back-East foreign. These people was from somewhere across the big water.

"What brings ya out here, Tirley?" the guide asked Pa. I looked the older man over again. His face was seamed with lifelines, but his eyes was sharp. He'd given no indication that he'd known Pa when we rode up.

"Me and the boy got tired of cows, so we're headin' fer the high country for a few weeks," Pa replied. He gestured to the fancy folks who had stepped away and were talking. "How'd you get hooked up with this bunch of pilgrims, Stoney?"

"Needed the money, and they needed a guide to show 'em how to hunt." The man replied simply. "Huntin' the American West is gettin' to be one of them things the Germans and English think is mighty important. The food's good. They brought a cook with 'em from one of the big hotels."

"Food's mighty important when you get to be our age," Pa said, smilin'. He looked down at me and pointed at the guide. "Matt, this here is Stone-Cold Phillips. We called him Stoney back in the old days." Pa saw my look and figured what was on my mind. The man had an uncommon name, and I reckoned it wasn't one he'd been born with.

"He got the name Stone-Cold when he was missin' from our camp on the Green," Pa explained. "We figured the Blackfeet had him stone-cold dead. He come draggin' in a few days later sproutin' a few arrows from his carcass and a little worse for wear. He weren't dead, but the name stuck."

Stone-Cold looked me over, and then looked back to Pa. "Looks like you been feedin' this boy good." I felt a flush come over my face.

"He is a big 'un," Pa agreed. "Biggest of the pack 'though my oldest boy is near that big."

"You be the Matt O'Malley I been hearin' about?" Stoney asked me.

"I don't know what you been hearin', but it's likely," I replied. "It's nothin' I've sought after."

Stoney nodded, apparently satisfied with my answer. He looked back over at Pa. "Heard you had a bit of trouble yourself over to Denver, Tirley."

"One of the men what killed my wife and burnt my place in the East whilst I was in the big fight," Pa said. He pushed back his buckskin sleeve and showed the scar. Stoney nodded, but said nothin'.

"You want any company on your hunt?" Stoney asked Pa.

Pa looked at me and then back to Stoney. "We ain't lookin' for company on this one, Stoney, but in a few weeks we hope to head over toward the Blues. Matt here is my partner, and you know the way with partners. I'd not say it was fine 'less he told me I could."

"You know I don't care, Pa," I said.

"I figured as much," Pa said. "You got anything against Mexicans?" he asked Stoney.

"They be humble folks, least the ones I've known, and if they like ya, they'll do anything for ya," Stoney said.

"We got a Mexican boy riding with us when we head west."

"Fine with me," Stoney said.

"When you get these folks headed home, go over to the ranch site 'bout a two-hour ride north and a little east. The rest of my boys are there. Me and Matt should be down in a week, maybe a little longer.''

Stoney smiled, spit a brown stream of tobacco on a passin' bug, and nodded. ''It'll be like old times.''

''Might not be as much fun. We won't have to duck the Blackfeet,'' Pa said with a smile.

We mounted up and headed for the high country. We camped just at dusk halfway up the Storm King next to a purty little stream of water.

Mornin' come on fine and sharp with a heavy dew, and after a breakfast of elk steaks, we headed on up the mountain with Pa leadin' the way.

I showed Pa the hidden trail to the top of Storm King, and he give out a mild swear word.

''All the times I been around here in the old days lookin' fer a way up, and it was right here all the time.''

''I can see how'd you'd miss it,'' I said. ''I watched Kurlow's men ride past it several times and not pick it out.''

We rode into the dark opening maybe a hundred feet, and Pa drew up.

''I'm gonna go hide our trail, Matt. I'll meet you on top.''

I nudged Sin, and he scrambled up the steep, sandy slope with the Morgan pullin' back on his lead rope. I broke out on top, pulled up, and stepped out of the saddle.

I walked to the rim and could see Pa below me blending the soft dirt and sand in a way that looked natural and covered our tracks. I looked farther out and reckoned I could nearly see the hind-end of the world from where I stood. We was high up, probably over ten thousand feet, and the air was clear and thin. I spotted a thin layer of dust hangin' in the air down toward the meadows. It might be elk, which weren't likely, or Injuns or even Kurlow. It paid a man to watch for things like that little wisp of dust. It could make all the difference in this country where a man could get hisself killed in a dozen different ways.

''An Injun would spot that, but not many white men,'' Pa said, talkin' about the place he'd covered our tracks.

I climbed back up onto Sin, and we sat there for quite a spell takin' in the country and not sayin' anythin'. The sun was warm on our backs, and it was right pleasant.

"There's a spread o' country out there," Pa finally said. "Don't reckon there's enough people in the world to fill it up."

"It's a purty sight," I said. "I like the mountain country."

"You was bred to it, boy. I come to these mountains when I was still just a cub, and I went places where no man had set a foot before. It were a great adventure, but dangerous. I near went under more times than I can count."

We were quiet again, and a raven croaked over near the red upthrust I'd called Hotel Rock.

"We'd best get a camp laid," Pa said. "Won't be long 'til the sun's down."

We turned and rode toward the center of the flat-topped mountain. I showed Pa the ground-down spot in the slick-rock, and then showed him the cave and the Spanish skeletons. He got down and walked into the cave, bein' careful not to disturb the skeletons.

"Nothin' in here 'less they buried it," Pa said, his voice echoing eerily from the rock walls. I had a shiver run over me and looked over my shoulder. I saw nothin', but I felt like I was bein' watched.

Pa come out and climbed back on his horse. "I'd as soon not camp too close around here," he said, speakin' what I was thinkin'. "I don't believe in haunts, but the Injuns say this mountain is surely haunted. No use messin' with stuff we know nothin' about." I was glad to hear him say it.

We found us a nice spot not far from the rim, but quite a ways from the Spanish cave and the Injun ruins as well. We saw to the horses and set up camp. There wasn't a breath of air movin', and it was so quiet you could've heard a bug break wind. The sun was down time we got situated, and the coffee smelled good on the little fire we'd built.

"It'll get cold up here tonight," Pa said. "I seen the time when country this high has got a foot of snow in June."

He grabbed the coffeepot off the fire and poured me a cup of coffee. It was darker than the inside of a black cow and strong enough to near melt a man's teeth.

"We'll scout a bit in the mornin', and see if we can figure where the Spanish boys was diggin'. We find their mine, we might find their cache as well," Pa said. He took a sip from his cup and rolled his lips back with satisfaction. "Now that I seen 'em, I figure you're right," he said. "Them Spaniards was killed 'fore they got the gold out." He took another sip of coffee from his beat-up tin cup and moved one of the elk steaks that he was broilin' to a different spot over the coals.

"From the looks of the hole they ground down over on the flat rock, I'd say they worked quite a bit of ore. They probably made some trips out, but they surely didn't make the last one."

"That was my thinkin'," I replied. "Even if there ain't much, anything'll help. We surely need the money."

"You know," Pa said, "I bet I've heard a hundred stories about lost Spanish mines. I never paid 'em no mind, figurin' they was mostly wishful thinkin'. I might have to try and remember some of 'em now that you showed me this."

We ate the steaks and then laid back on our blankets lookin' at the stars. We never said a word for an hour, just watchin' and thinkin'. My eyes was gettin' heavy, so I lifted the tarp that I always laid over my blankets and crawled in. Pa was breathin' in long heavy strokes, so I reckoned he'd gone on to sleep. It was nice bein' with Pa. He was teachin' me things without even knowin' he was doin' it. I watched the way he put a fire together with almost no effort and the way he found a campsite that had all the things that made a man comfortable. He could track a fly across a rock, make his way through the bushes without a sound, and read the sky and tell you when a storm was comin'. They was things that come natural to him as wearin' his skin. He knew more about wild country than anybody I ever seen. I was glad we'd taken this ride even if we found no gold. It was time I needed with Pa.

I looked over at the coals of the dyin' fire, and all of a sudden a gust of wind come up. A tiny flame popped out, and I could hear somethin' off in the distance. Sin's head come up like it was on springs, and I looked over to Pa's bed. He weren't there.

"Lay easy, boy," Pa said from the darkness by the big cedar tree. "It's a habit of mine. I sleep light, and I'm quick out of the blankets."

The wind stirred again, and I heard the noise, soft but still there.

"It's just the wind," Pa said as he stepped back to his blankets.

I reached up and made sure my short gun was close to hand. It might've just been the wind, but I was certain sure that I'd heard voices, and it sounded like they was talkin' Spanish.

Chapter Fifteen

" "That's where they was diggin', sure," Pa said.

We was standin' maybe two hundred yards from the spot where the Spanish had milled their ore. Pa had got to talkin' over breakfast and reckoned that the mine would have to be somewhere fairly close to the mill. He'd been right.

We'd hiked to the mill spot, and Pa started lookin' about. It wasn't long 'til he'd found the trail cut into the soil of the mountaintop. The track was probably over three hundred years old, and it was purty hard to trace out in places. Pa showed me where they'd cut off a cedar tree that stood in their way and another spot where they'd chipped steps for the mules up onto a rock ledge. We followed the trail until we finally come to a sudden rock upheaval. It was different from the rest of the rock found on top of the mountain. It was black, and looked like it'd been burnt by the fires of hell. It was big, maybe a hundred feet tall, and not much wider than that. There was a hole right at the bottom of it.

There was a few crude tools lyin' at the base of the upheaval and a small, badly weathered pannier handmade out of cedar. We stepped down from the horses, loose-tied 'em to a wind-blasted pinyon tree, and walked over to the shaft.

"Not much of a mine by today's reckonin'," Pa said. "Big man have trouble gettin' into it."

Me and Pa was both bigger than the regular fella, and I had no urge to crawl into the hole. Trouble was, I knew we had to do it.

"I 'spect I can get into it if I suck my wind in," I said.

"You'll need a torch," Pa said, not tryin' to talk me out of it like I'd hoped. He walked over to a pinyon tree and found a limb that had fallen off. The knot part of it was still hooked on, and it was full of pitch. He got it lit with little trouble, and it give off a smoke as black as the rock I was crawlin' into.

"I don't reckon there's many snakes out up here yet. Still too cold. That hole would make a purty nice place fer rattlers to winter in if it's very deep. I'd keep an eye open if'n I was you."

"Thanks, Pa. That makes me feel a whole lot better," I said. He grinned at me, and I walked up to the dark opening of the hole. It was maybe five and a half feet high by four feet. I bent over and stepped in. The shaft pointed down kinda steep, but not so bad that I had trouble keepin' my feet under me. I walked down a slow step at a time for maybe fifteen steps, and the shaft leveled off. It widened out a little, but didn't get no taller. I was still all bent over, and my breath was comin' in short little puffs.

I walked maybe fifty feet 'til I could see the end of the shaft ahead of me. There was a stark white quartz seam that come up from the floor and stopped just short of the ceilin'. I was certain the quartz was what they'd been diggin' out. From the length of the shaft I reckoned they must have worked at it for quite a spell. I walked up close to the seam and held the torch to it. I couldn't see anything in the quartz that looked like gold, but I weren't no judge. I looked around and couldn't see any loose ore or anything else that looked like a cache. I managed to get turned around and made better time gettin' out than I had goin' in. When I broke out into the sunlight, I took a deep breath of fresh air. I was downright glad to see the sky over me, and it felt good to stand up straight.

"There's a seam of quartz at the back of the hole. It ain't very wide but runs from the bottom of the hole clear to the ceilin'." I took another deep breath. "It's tight, but not as bad as it looks from out here."

Pa took the torch from me and went into the hole. He come back out in five minutes and threw the torch on the sand.

"Don't look like there's much gold in the quartz, but I don't know that much 'bout it," he said. "We'd need some powder, drills, and hammers to check it for certain. We'd probably be better off lookin' for a cache of stuff that's already dug out.''

''Where you reckon they'd put it?'' I asked.

''If'n it was me, I'd a put it over toward the cave they was shelterin' in, but them boys didn't think like we do. It might be 'bout anywheres, if there is any.''

''Let's go back over to the skeleton cave and look around a little more. Maybe we can see somethin' more today than we saw last evenin','' I suggested. I had no great urge to mess around them dead men again, but if the gold was up here, I meant to find it.

We rode over to the shelter and walked over to the low wall that ran along the front of the big opening and looked in. They was still there and didn't look like they'd moved any. I don't know what I expected, but I was a mite skittish rememberin' the talkin' wind of the night before.

''They didn't die easy,'' Pa said in a quiet voice.

We stepped over the wall and walked into the shelter. The cave was like many Western caves. It'd been carved by the sand pushed by the wind for centuries. It was tall, rounded, and wide. It wasn't very deep, and we could clearly see the back. There were frames made from smoothed cedar for beds, and bits and pieces of clothing spread about. Most of it was rotted, and the leather items were shrunken and cracked. They'd lived rough, but they was used to it.

''Matt,'' Pa said. He'd walked off a ways to the other side of the cave, and he was pointin' at the back wall.

''What's that mean?'' I asked. He was pointin' at a Spanish Cross that had been chipped into the face of the rock. It was about six feet off the ground with the long part of the cross pointin' to the ceilin'. I looked up, and I could see a narrow ledge that stuck out from the rock face. Without the cross pointin' up, I'd've never noticed it. I looked at Pa, and he had an excited look on his face.

''It's up there, Matt. I know it is.''

My heart beat a little faster, and I felt the excitement build in my gut.

"How do we get up there?" I asked.

"Same way they did. We'll have to build us a ladder."

We went back out into the bright sunlight and started lookin' for poles we could use for the uprights. It took us most of two hours to build the ladder. We cut a bunch of crosspieces from cedar limbs and tied them to the uprights with rawhide that Pa had brought along. After a while we had a ladder, of sorts, and carried it into the cave. The ladder was wobbly after we got it propped up, and it was a mite short.

"I'll go up, Pa," I said. The sand in the bottom of the cave was soft, and I figured if the ladder fell I could take the bounce better than Pa.

"Keep your feet up close to the edge of the rungs," he advised. "There's more support to the edges than in the middle."

I started climbin' up, holding some of my weight with my hands and tryin' to step light. I got near the top, and the ladder was groanin' and developin' a bow in the middle. I was barely breathin', and my pucker string was pulled up tight. The top rung come even with my eyes and I could still barely reach the ledge. I was gonna have to go at least one step higher. I stepped up onto the next crosspiece, makin' the rawhide bindings creak with my weight. I grabbed the ledge with my hand and pulled myself up with the strength of my arms.

The Spanish boys had been purty sly. They'd deepened the hole behind the ledge and put up a little masonry wall back out of sight of the ground. I crawled in deeper and saw the buckskin bags layin' in neat rows.

"It's here, Pa," I yelled down. "Stand back and I'll throw one down." My voice echoed from the ceiling and sounded hollow to my ears.

I grabbed one of the bags. They weren't very big, but they was heavy. I looked down, saw Pa was clear, and dropped the bag over. It split when it hit, and Pa scrambled over to it.

"It's been milled, Matt. It's rich, and purty free of quartz. I'd say there's five hundred dollars worth in this bag. Is this more?"

"Nine more bags just like that one," I hollered down. There

wasn't as much as I'd hoped for, but it was enough. It would see the partnership though 'til we was ready to sell beef.

I dropped 'em over one at a time. I threw the last one down and looked hard toward the back of the ledge to see if I'd missed any. It was purty dark, but I could see somethin' shinin'. I reached as far back as I could and touched somethin' cold. I pulled it out and sucked in my air. It was a Spanish sword, and a showy one at that. The handle was set all in gold and jewels, and there was some fancy letterin' on the blade. I didn't want to drop the sword, so I pushed it up close to the ladder where I could grab it.

I let myself down to the ladder, caught hold of the sword, and headed down.

''I brought some flour sacks with me,'' Pa said, as he walked back into the cave from outside. ''We can use them to carry the gold and spread the load out over the four horses.''

He stopped when he saw the sword in my hand. It was big, there weren't a speck of rust on it, and it was sharp both blade and point. It was meant to be used, not just carried.

''That's a purty piece, Matt. A real craftsman made that, and it didn't belong to just any ol' Spanish piker. That's a nobleman's sword.''

We made short work of scoopin' the gold into the flour sacks, and we sifted the sand in our hands makin' sure we got all the little chunks loaded.

''Let's carry it over to the front of the cave, then we can bring the horses up here,'' Pa suggested.

''Seems like a plan to me,'' I agreed. The sacks were heavy, and I had no hankerin' to carry 'em too far.

It took us most of the rest of the mornin' to get the gold loaded and our camp stuff packed up. Time we finished, the horses was fair loaded. We figured we'd have to camp one more night on the mountain, but farther down.

We ate a quick meal of jerky washed down with coffee, then we swung onto our horses and pointed 'em toward the hidden trail. We'd rode for a short distance, and I pulled up.

"I need to go back over to the Spanish cave for a minute, Pa. I left that sword back toward the ladder."

"I'd plumb forgot about it," Pa said. "I don't think anybody will find it, but no use takin' the chance. It's too fine a piece to leave up here."

We turned back and rode to the cave. A sharp gust of wind come up and near blew my hat off, and Pa grabbed for his badger just as it lifted off. We tied the horses off to the tree again, and both of us walked into the cave. I walked over to the ladder and grabbed up the sword where I'd leaned it against the back wall. I picked it up in my left hand and liked the weight of it. It was perfectly balanced and must've been some Spanish man's pride and joy. I walked over to the skeletons and looked 'em over one more time.

"They done fine by us, boy," Pa said. "We owe 'em some thanks."

"That we do," I agreed.

"Well, what we got here?" The deep booming voice came from behind us. It was such a shock to hear a strange voice that I jumped. Pa and me turned at the same time. They had their guns on us. There was four of 'em, and one of 'em was an Injun. They had us fair trapped, and they knew it.

The man talkin' had a grin on his face, and I could tell he was some pleased with hisself.

"We were comin' down from the old stone cabin on the other side of the mountain toward evenin' yesterday and seen your smoke. The Digger found where you'd covered your trail," he said, pointin' to the Injun. "Nate Kurlow and Daniel Briggs put together quite a force, and we was aimin' to catch you all at the ranch and wipe you out."

"I thought Briggs had headed for California," I said. I wanted to keep the conversation goin'. Me and Pa was in trouble, and we needed some kind of edge.

"He wanted everybody to think he'd gone to California. He's leadin' up the little army we put together and doin' a fine job of it," the man bragged. "Him and Kurlow planned on takin' the ranch all along, but the timin' had to be right."

"What makes the time right now?" I asked.

"The Army is chasin' some Apaches down toward the pueblos, which only leaves only you and yours that we have to deal with. Shouldn't be much of a job."

They was sure of themselves. Maybe too sure. I figured me and Pa was gonna die right here where the Spanish boys had, but we was gonna make a fight of it.

"Briggs figured it was either part of your clan or Injuns up here on top, and the renegades had told us all that no Injun would come up here. I can see why now," he said gesturing toward the dead Spaniards. "They say it's haunted, and after we get done, there's gonna be two more ghosts walkin' around." He had a wolfish grin on his face, and I knew he was working himself up to it.

Pa had managed to edge away from me, putting a little distance between us, which give us a better chance. I figured the time for talkin' was over. We was just about to have us a fight, and some of us were gonna die.

Chapter Sixteen

A gust of strong wind hit us again makin' the sand blow around our ankles. As the wind hit the back wall of the cave it set up a terrible moanin'. It was what we'd heard the night before, and the men in front of us glanced toward the back of the cave. I shucked my Colt and shot into the talkin' man, makin' the dust jump from his vest. I turned slightly and shot the man in the middle three times as fast as I could slip the hammer. I heard Pa's gun workin', and I shot the talkin' man again as he fell. His gun went off into the sand at his feet, and the man beside him fell on top of him. I turned my head quickly to look at the Injun, but he was runnin'. I could see him just goin' into the cedars, and he was in a full-out sprint.

Pa ran to the horses and grabbed his Hawken from the boot. He stepped out from behind his horse, raised the rifle, took a deep breath, and then shot. The Injun left his feet like he'd been hit with a giant fist, and then lay motionless. It was one of the finest shots I'd ever seen.

I looked at the men in front of me. Pa had shot one of the outlaws through the brisket. He and the two I'd taken on was as dead as the Spanish boys layin' around us.

"We'd best get to the ranch," I said. "We're gonna be too late, but maybe they can hold 'em off 'til we get there."

Pa didn't say a word. He just run to the horses and climbed up. I'd shoved the sword down in my rifle scabbard with my Henry.

"We'll drop the gold off after we get down the slot," Pa said, "along with everything else. We got to make time, and we can't do it with loaded horses."

He turned his horse's head toward the hidden trail and kicked him in the ribs. He took off like shot from a cannon, and I was right on his heels. We blasted down the slot and pulled up in the soft sand at the bottom of the cliff face.

"Drop everything off both horses," Pa yelled. "Turn the pack-horses loose. They'll follow us down."

In half a heartbeat we was in the saddle again. We hit the main trail and turned toward the ranch. I was some scared for our folks down there. They wouldn't be expectin' the attack.

It was a wild ride. We slid in the steep spots, jumped over down trees in the trail, and got beat half to death by branches. I looked over my shoulder from time to time to see how Pa was doin'. He was keepin' up with me, but he'd lost his hat, and he had an angry-looking welt on his face where he'd been raked by a branch. His white hair was streamin' out behind him, and his eyes was wild. I reckoned he looked just like the Irishers that had fought the Brits in the old days.

It took us near two hours to get off the mountain, and the horses was some tired when we made the meadows. We pulled up a ways out from the buildings. There was no gunfire, and I could see several bodies layin' in the yard.

I took my Henry from the boot, makin' sure the sword stayed put, and we walked the horses in quiet and easy. My heart was in my throat. There was no question we was too late. There was maybe twenty bodies layin' out in the open, and none of 'em was movin'.

I heard the door open on the big cabin, and I swung in the saddle to cover it with my Henry.

"Everyone's okay, Matt. They are gone, or at least the ones that could still ride." It was Shadrach Taylor, and he was sporting a new federal badge on his chest. Both Meshach and Abendigo followed on his heels.

I started lookin' at the bodies layin' in the yard and realized I didn't know any of 'em. They must've been with Kurlow's outlaws.

I heard the sounds of horses and tack jinglin', and a troop of Cavalry come ridin' from around the barn. They pulled up, and

I seen Danny. He come ridin' over as I stepped down from my horse.

"I'd guess you'd say that Briggs and Kurlow made a misjudgment," Dan said. "The Cavalry is from Fort Lewis, and they were huntin' some renegades over this direction. They stopped here to water and eat rations." He pointed to the three federal marshals standing shoulder to shoulder on the porch. "The Taylor boys had information on Briggs that said he planned on hittin' us here at the ranch. They showed up the morning you left. Stone-Cold Phillips came in the same time the Taylors did. He said he'd been invited to go along on a trek with you and Pa over to the Blues, and Chris Silva got back the pueblos yesterday." Dan stopped talkin' a minute and looked about him and then rubbed Sin on the neck. "With Uncle John, Holstein Tommy, and the ranch hands we have something over fifty guns, and every one of them knows how to shoot. We even had some warning before they hit us. Billy Dean was up in the meadows looking for a calf and saw the bandits riding down through the trees. He knew who they were and came back here shootin' and screamin' all the way. By the time Kurlow's bunch got within rifle range, the Army was up and ready for them, as were the rest of us. We waited until they got into the yard where we had them in a crossfire, and cut 'em down."

"We lose anybody?" Pa asked. He'd ridden up beside us and was still sittin' his horse.

"Wedge has got a real painful wound, but not too dangerous. He was just running into the barn and a stray shot took him in the rump. It kinda skidded across and laid him open. He's not in the best of humor." Dan pointed to the bodies that lay scattered around. "We counted twenty-three here, and there are five or six down by the creek and out in the meadows. Stoney was shooting a brand-new Sharps he said some German gave him. The darn thing will shoot nearly to Denver. He did for most of them out a distance."

"Kurlow?" I asked.

"He's not among the dead," Danny said. "There was three or four that cut and run early, so I figure he was one of them."

"What about Daniel Briggs?" Pa asked.

Uncle John come out of the main cabin holdin' a piece of flour sack to his face. When he took it down, I noticed one eye was swollen up, and he had a cut on his cheek.

"Our hunt's over, Pa," Danny said. "Briggs got knocked off his horse and ended up on foot. Uncle John whipped Briggs 'til he couldn't stand. He's the only one of the gang we took alive. He's over in the grainery in chains." Danny pointed over to the squat log building that has no windows and only one little door. "The Taylors plan on takin' him back to Denver, and then on to Washington to stand trial just as soon as you confirm he's Dunn."

I walked Sin to the barn just as the Morgan came into the yard along with Pa's packhorse. They came right to the barn and buried their noses in the water trough outside the door.

Billy Dean came out and took Sin from me.

"I'll take of him, Matt," Billy said. "He needs to be rubbed down, and looks like his legs need attention."

I walked down to the creek and looked out across the meadows. Owen came down and stood close by. The Army and most of the rest of our folks was gatherin' up horses, pickin' up fallen guns, and liftin' the bodies into our wagons. The place surely looked like a battlefield.

"Lot of folks died," I said, mostly to myself.

"Probably be a lot more people die before this land is settled," Owen said. He'd been readin' law and talked some about doin' some politickin'. His speech had got better, and he'd got to be a thinker. I reckoned it was good that one of us boys was thinkin'. The rest of us seemed to react more than we thought.

"There's times when I wonder if all the killin' is worth it," I said.

Owen got a surprised look on his face. "Matthew, where's the man that helped build a town from creek mud and prairie out in Kansas? Where's the man that fought off Comanches, renegades, outlaws, and all others that come against us, and did it because he was tryin' to build something worthwhile? You've told me more than once that you'd fight to the death for our homes and the right to live as free men."

Owen was near yellin' when he got done, and his face was red.

"He's right, boy." It was Pa. He'd come behind us while we was talkin'.

"You heard me say it a thousand times while we was all home on the farm together. Your home is always worth fightin' for. If you let down your guard, then the bad ones get strong, and soon decent folks can't live in peace." He leaned over and with a cupped hand scooped up some water from the creek. The water ran through his fingers as he held his hand up.

"Happiness and freedom are just like the water in my hand. They're hard to hold to, but like water, a man has a hard time livin' without 'em. Believe me, Matthew, when I tell ya that they are ideals worth fightin' and even dyin' for."

"I do, Pa," I said. "I've even said things like that before, wonderin' where I'd learned it. Now I know."

"This frontier is no different that any other frontier in the world, either now, or in the past. Frontiers are won with men's blood. It has always been so and always will be," Owen said.

"From the stories I heard my grandpap tell, I believe the O'Malleys have always left blood at the front of new lands. We O'Malleys, both men and women, have always been at the head of the drive lookin' at new places and seekin' our fortunes in strange lands. It's bred to us."

"We have a new home here," Danny said. He and Mike had come walkin' down from the buildings when they saw us gathered at the creek. "Somethin' I learned over the years is that most times the sweetest things in a man's life are the ones he's fought for."

"The fight may be against enemies, like this was, or nature like we did last winter or even with ourselves to learn the discipline that it takes to overcome what stands in our way. A man's life is a fight from the beginning to the end, and what counts is how he faced the battle," Owen added.

"The O'Malleys have had outlaws in their past, accordin' to Grandpap," Pa added, "but even them was made because of politics, and they was fightin' for what they figured was right."

"We won't all of us stay here in this valley," Owen said, "But we will always have the Storm King as our home. It is a place to return to, a place where we became a family once again." Owen looked around at us one by one. "We talked some while you and Pa were up on the mountain," he said, resting his eyes on me. "Patty wants me to be a lawyer and maybe go into politics. It's what I'd like as well. The Taylor boys want Danny to go with them and join up as a lawman. Mike wants to stay with the ranch, as does Wedge and Jessie. Uncle John is heading back for Denver and his business holdings. I don't know what you want, Matt, but you're young yet. You have a lot of life in front of you."

"Me, Matt, Chris, and Stoney are goin' trekkin', and when we come back, I'm goin' up on Thunder Mountain and live in my cabin. I'll hunt, trap, and come down to the meadows when I get a hankerin' for company. Least my boys will be close, and I'll have the mountains around me. This is where I'll finish out," Pa said.

"Matt . . . ?" There was a question in Owen's voice.

"I don't know," I said. "If Lee was here, it'd be all different. I'd probably stick right close and raise me a family. With her lost to me . . . I just don't know." I looked at the wagon as it headed for the cemetery, and looked back to my family. "I can tell you one thing. None of us are safe until Nate Kurlow is either dead or behind bars. We ain't seen the last of him."

We walked toward the cabins, quiet now, each of us lost in our own thoughts. It looked like we was gonna split up again, but at least this time it wasn't a war makin' the decision for us.

Pa stopped sudden and looked over at us. "Think I'll go see me a man," he said.

"Mind if we come along?" Danny asked.

"No, I reckon not. This is part your job anyhow," Pa replied.

We walked over to the grainery, and Pa lifted up the bar that held the door closed. Light flooded into the dark interior, and the man inside blinked his eyes against the brightness. His arms and legs was held in chains that rattled as he stood. Uncle John had made his marks on him, some he'd carry to the grave. He was a big man with dark hair but had a whipped look about him.

"Well, O'Malley, you've been a curse on me since the day you showed up in Grant's camp," the man said when he spotted Pa.

"You had choices you made, Dunn. Weren't all my doin'," Pa replied.

"From the first time I heard your name, I had it on my mind to kill you. Now you've cost me my career, my money, my reputation, and probably my life. I won't last long in prison." He stopped talkin' a minute and looked behind us. I turned and saw Uncle John had come walkin' up.

"The same with you," Dunn continued, lookin' at John. "I'd thought I could get at Tirley through you, knowing how the O'Malleys are about family."

"What was your purpose?" John asked.

"I've hated all the O'Malleys since I was a boy. I didn't know exactly why then, but it was drilled into me. My mother schooled me in the things the O'Malleys had done to my family over the years." Dunn moved a step forward with his chains rattling. His face was full of hate and loathing. I'd never seen a man so full of malice in all my life.

"My mother's name was Martha Kurlow before she married James Dunn," he said. "Nathan Kurlow is my nephew. We were born to hate you . . . hate you all."

Pa closed the door on him, and we walked away. The things he'd said went a long ways toward explainin' what had happened over the past several months.

The next week went fast as we cleaned up the ranch, started brandin' new calves with the O bar M, and commenced gettin' ready for the trek. I was some excited about travelin'. I had it on me to see some new sights.

Pa and Stoney had gone back to the top of the mountain and gathered up the gold. I knew when we'd told the partnership about us findin' the Spanish gold, there had been a collective sigh of relief. It made things look a sight better. Neither Pa nor me mentioned the hole in the volcanic rock. It was in our minds to go back up some day.

It was two days and a week after the fight. I was short on rounds for my Henry, and Chris and I'd decided to ride down to the little town of Saguache and gather up a few other things we needed for the ride West. Owen had convinced me to take the Spanish sword I'd found into town and let John Lawrence have a look at it. He had a reputation as something of a scholar, and we was all curious about it.

It was a bright, warm mornin' when we rode down the single street of the town. It had grown little since I'd last been in. Most everyone still knew me by sight and called out a greeting. We bought near all of our supplies now from Saguache, and they welcomed the business. It was a town on the edge of nowhere, strugglin' to survive. Otto Mears had a tradin' post where you could find most of what a man needed in this country. He was a little man, some said a Jew, with some kind of accent, who had a fire in his belly to make big tracks. When he got to the site there was three white families and about the same number of Spanish descent.

I'd always got on good with Mears and the other folks of Saguache as well. They was hardworking, humble folks, and they treated both Chris and me with respect.

"Ah, it is Matthew O'Malley and Christian Silva," Otto said as I walked into the interior of the trading post. There was two small Ute boys standin' to one side of the counter lookin' at the penny candy. It wasn't unusual to see Utes in Saguache. Otto Mears and the tribe got on well, and he had learned to speak Ute. "We have heard about your fight at the ranch. There are too many outlaws in the country."

"Speakin' of which, I need some cartridges for my Henry," I said.

"I have three boxes I ordered in just for you," Otto said. "They are in the back," he pointed to a door at the back of the store. The little man bustled out just as John Lawrence came into the store. He was a distinguished-lookin' man and every inch a gentleman.

"Mr. Lawrence, I was just gonna go see if I could find you. I got somethin' I'd like to have you eyeball."

"Very well, Matthew. I was just coming in to see if Otto had any more of his fine smoking tobacco."

"I got it out on my horse," I said, moving toward the front door. I walked over to Sin and drawed the sword from the rifle boot on my saddle. I'd wrapped it in a thin oilcloth for protection. I unwrapped and admired the sword for a second in the sunlight and walked back to the store.

I handed it to John Lawrence, and he sucked in his wind. "Where did you find this, Matthew?" he asked me. I trusted Mr. Lawrence, but I wasn't about to go spoutin' off.

"It was around our ranch," I said, which was mostly true.

Lawrence looked at me, smiled, and turned his attention back to the sword. "It is probably thirteenth-century Spanish in origin." He turned it over in his hands and then handed it back to me. "It is said that Chris Columbus had a sword much like that given to him by Isabella. The royalty bestowed them upon special people of the realm."

"Would you like to sell it, Matthew?" Otto asked me. He'd come in from the back room and laid my shells on the counter.

"I reckon not, Mr. Mears. Least not right now."

I saw movement from the corner of my eye, and looked out the front door.

"Chris," I said in a low voice. He stepped up next to me, then slipped the keeper from his pistol. I checked both of my pistols, and then looked back to Mears and Lawrence.

"I'd reckon you might want to hunker down behind the counter and wait 'til this is over." My tone was even, but that surely wasn't what I was feelin'. Across the street from the store stood Nate Kurlow and several men. They surely recognized my horse. They were waitin' for me to come out. I'd ridden to the little town of Saguache, and trouble had surely found me.

Chapter Seventeen

" "I will go out the back, amigo," Chris said.

"Here, take this, Silva," Mr. Lawrence offered. "It's loaded to kill deer." He handed Chris a shotgun, then turned back to me. "Don't go out there, Matt. You don't stand a chance."

"I have it to do," I said. "Kurlow declared a blood feud, and he'll stand by it."

I walked toward the front door and started toward the six men standin' across the narrow street. I looked down and saw I still had the Spanish sword in my hand. I dropped it in the dust to free my hand for my gun. I stopped and looked at the man I had grown to hate.

"The time has come, O'Malley," he said. The scar on his face was livid, and he had a terrible look about him.

"I reckon it has," I replied and drew my right-hand gun before any of 'em was ready. I shot Kurlow first. I knew instinctively that my shot had been true, but it didn't seem to affect him. I heard a shotgun boom from behind me as I triggered three more shots so fast they sounded like one continuous roar. Men across from me were falling onto the ground as I shot. Kurlow had vanished, but I had no time to look about for him. It surely sounded like a thousand guns were bein' fired on my side of the street. I hammered my last shot into a fat man with a florid face and drew my belt gun. I fired until there was no one left standin' in front of me. It got deathly still as the shootin' stopped. All the outlaws was lyin' on the ground either wounded or dead, except Kurlow.

Movement to my left caught my attention, and I saw him. He'd run to his horse, but he weren't tryin' to climb up. Instead he

179

jerked a Shoshone war ax from behind his saddle and come run-nin' for me swingin' the ax. I wondered why he wasn't usin' his gun, but didn't take long to think on it. My short guns were all empty, and my Henry was still on Sin. I knew how fast and deadly Kurlow was in this kind of fight. He'd near got me in the cabin fight.

"Matt," I turned my head slightly as Chris called my name. He tossed me the Spanish sword, and I caught it by the haft in my right hand. I turned back just as Kurlow rushed up to me. He took a mighty swing with the ax, and I was hard pressed to dodge him. He was lithe and quick, and if I'd hit him with that first pistol shot he showed no signs of it. I parried a strong blow with the sword, and it rung out as he hit it with the iron of the ax.

Kurlow walked toward me slow, lookin' for an opening. As he come close, I took a quick shuffle step forward and slashed at him. The sword was wonderfully balanced, and I near got him. His speed saved him, but it was close, and he got more cautious. He rushed again, choppin' like a wild man and screamin'. I parried him blow for blow and took another slice at him. I grazed him across the chest, and he stepped back, blood seepin' from the cut.

I moved in on him fast and pressed him hard. He was good, and I couldn't get a clear hack at him. Sweat was startin' to run down my face, and we was kickin' the dry ground of the street into a stiflin' dust. My breath was comin' in great gulps, and I was scared. I surely didn't want to die here on this dusty street.

He come at me again, screamin' and swingin' so fast I couldn't track all his moves. He swung at me backhand and hit me with the flat of the blade on the shoulder. It knocked me down, and I knew he'd be on me. I rolled away as fast as I could and got to my knees. I stopped a tremendous blow with the sword and coun-tered with a slash as he recocked. He saw it comin' and turned away from me with a spin move. I opened him up a little on the back. It was deeper than the chest wound, but still not enough.

He come at me again so hard I tripped over my own feet and fell onto my back. I rolled just in time to cause a mighty blow directed at my head to miss. The ax buried into the dirt of the street, and I punched Nathan with my left fist right on the scar I'd given him. He screamed in my face. He was completely gone out of his head.

I rolled again and got to my knees. I needed to get my feet under me, or I was surely gonna die. He come on a dead run, and I knew I wasn't gonna stop him this time. I grabbed the sword by the haft and threw it the way that the Utes threw their lances. I was scared, and I threw the sword hard, hopin' to divert him 'til I could get my feet under me. It hit him pointfirst, true as any spear, and stuck clear up to the jeweled handle. He had a surprised look on his face. Probably nearly as surprised as me. He fell onto his side, and the war ax dropped to the ground.

I walked over to him and looked at his pistol, which was in his holster. The action was smashed. I figured I hit it with my first shot when the fight started.

''My brothers . . .'' he whispered.

I leaned over so to hear him, and he whispered again. ''My brothers will . . .'' and then he was gone.

I ought to say I was sorry, but I weren't. Nathan Kurlow had chosen his path, and he had died on the dusty streets of a small Colorado town. A year down the road nobody but me would even remember his name.

I got my sword, and looked around. Most of the male population of Saguache was standin' about me. They all had various kinds of guns in their hands, and I knew that the outlaws had died not realizin' the mistake they'd made comin' to Saguache to make trouble. There might not be a lawman close to hand, but every townsman was either wearin' a gun or had one in his house, and they knew how to shoot. It gave me a warm feelin' knowin' the town had stood with me.

''You are okay, *señor?*'' Chris asked me.

I checked myself over and realized I wasn't bleedin' anywhere. ''I'm fine,'' I said, some surprised. ''You?''

''I am well,'' he replied.

''Guess I'll get my shells now, Mr. Mears,'' I said. He was standin' to the side of me, and the Smith & Wesson Russian he held in his hand still had a curl of smoke comin' from the barrel.

Mr. Lawrence was on the other side, and he was holdin' a Spencer. The townsmen drifted away one by one talkin' among themselves, and the mortician got busy linin' up the bodies. He was gonna be busy for a spell.

I saw two horsemen come bustin' around the curve that led to the main street of the town. I'd reloaded both my pistols, and I made sure they was ready. The fight might not be over after all. As the riders got closer I recognized Danny and Marshal Shadrach Taylor. They was dust covered and their horses was some lathered up. They slid to a stop beside me.

"Matt?" Danny said, lookin' at the outlaws' bodies.

"I'm fine, but Kurlow ain't so good." He was still layin' where we finished our fight.

"That Sutler from Garland came fogging into the ranch and said that Kurlow had been there last evening. He was making war talk and said he was hunting you," Dan said.

"He found me," I replied.

"Briggs finally told us that Kurlow had the government gold with him. Have you seen a wagon anywhere?"

"That's their wagon," John Lawrence said, pointin' to a spring wagon that was parked by a tree. He and Mears walked into the store, and we walked over to the wagon. Under a square of tarp in the bed of the wagon we found a strongbox marked U.S. ARMY. Inside was quite a stack of newly minted gold coin. I reckoned that General Grant would be plumb pleased to get his money back. From this point on it looked like a job for the marshal.

I walked over to the store, and Me and Chris finished gatherin' our supplies. We paid Otto, and I turned to him and John as we walked out of the store.

"I want to thank you—"

John Lawrence raised his hand and stopped me.

"We did it for ourselves as much as you, Matthew. We want the outlaws along the back trails to know that Saguache won't tolerate them. This story will be told for years around the campfires and in the saloons. I expect this fight will help make this town a peaceful and happy place to live."

We climbed up on our horses, and Shadrach got on the wagon.

He'd tied his horse on behind. Him and Dan had decided to go on to Denver with the government gold. I waved at Mears and Lawrence and turned Sin's head toward the ranch. We was just about to leave town when I stopped and turned to look back down the street. The mortician was still busy, but he was makin' slow work of it. Nathan Kurlow still lay where he had died.

"What did he say to you?" Chris asked.

"He said something about his brothers," I replied. "I didn't catch it all."

They'd been gone for two days when the man rode into the yard. Dan walked out to meet him.

"There a Matt O'Malley around here?" the man asked.

"I'm his brother, Dan O'Malley."

"Close enough," the dusty rider said. "I'm headin' over to the pueblos. The postmaster at Fort Garland asked if I'd ride over here and deliver this letter." He handed a battered envelope to Danny, and then walked his horse over to the water trough.

The envelope was addressed to Matthew O'Malley of the Storm King Ranch. It was a woman's handwriting.

"What is it, Danny?" Mike said, as he came walking up.

"It's a letter to Matt. Looks to be from Boston."

"You think it's from Lee?"

"I don't know, but it's likely. Matt doesn't know anybody in Boston."

Owen had seen the rider from the cabin porch. He walked over and took the letter as Dan handed it to him.

"Think we ought to open it?" Mike asked.

"Probably," Owen said. "Matt won't care."

Owen opened the envelope carefully, unfolded the paper, and began to read in a quiet voice.

Dearest Matthew:

This is the first letter I have ever written. I was ashamed to tell you before that I couldn't read or write. My aunt, Edna Wilkes, has secured a tutor for me, and I have studied hard. She has also taught me how to be a lady.

I went to Washington this past week and saw Ara Turbeck in a play. We had a long talk, and I now understand what happened. I thought you still loved her because she is so beautiful and such a great lady. That is the reason I left. I wanted to become a lady. I wanted to make sure you would never be ashamed of me.

I am not sorry I came to Boston. I am sorry for the way I left, but I have learned so much here that I can't feel remorse for making the trip.

I am coming home, Matt. I like Boston, but I miss Colorado. I miss the horses, the yells of the cowhands, the scent of fresh bread, and the smell of the pines on the mountain. Most of all, I miss you, Matthew O'Malley. . . .''

Owen looked up from the letter. ''The rest of it is stuff that Matt probably just as soon we didn't read, nor Lee either for that matter.''

Danny looked toward the San Juans that loomed like a giant wall to the West. ''If that letter had just come two days earlier,'' he said.

All three of the brothers looked to the west and wondered where Matt was, and when he'd be coming home.